First shock was when Phil's door was opened by his mum saying, "Ah, here she is at last. Thought you two had got lost."

I looked round assuming she was talking to someone behind me. But she wasn't. Yet, how could she expect me . . . We solemnly shook hands. Her lips smiled, her eyes bored into me and she said, "I've heard so much about you, Denise. Would you like a nice cup of tea?"

Resisting a temptation to say, "No, I'd like a nasty one", I just nodded my head. Anything to get rid of her. She scared me.

"Take Denise through to the lounge," she said to Phil. Then she lowered her voice and said all confidingly, "We don't normally use the lounge during the day but as this is rather a special occasion . . ." She gave a false laugh while a grinning Phil led me through a time warp.

The room was cluttered up with chairs Noah had probably sat on and sitting on one of them was someone who looked even older than Noah.

"Grandad, meet Denise."

The old guy creaked to life, stood up and raised his hand as if he were giving a salute. Then I realized I was supposed to shake hands. "He's a good boy, young Philip," he said gripping my hand. For an old man he had a very firm grip.

Pete Johnson

Secrets from the School Underground

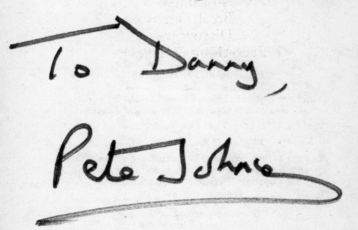

To Danny,

Pete Johnson

Mammoth

First published in Great Britain 1986
by André Deutsch Ltd
Published 1993 by Mammoth
an imprint of Reed Consumer Books Ltd
Michelin House, 81 Fulham Road, London SW3 6RB
and Auckland, Melbourne, Singapore and Toronto

Reprinted 1994 (twice)

ISBN 0 7497 1271 6

A CIP catalogue record for this title
is available from the British Library

Printed and bound in Great Britain
by Cox & Wyman Ltd, Reading, Berkshire

To – Janetta, Linda, Dodie Smith and all my friends from Sir William Ramsey School, Hazlemere, Bucks and Stevenage College.
With love – and thanks

Start Here

Want to show you something. Don't get too worked-up –
it's a wall. Smokers' Wall. You'll find it by the bike sheds at
Farndale School. Twice a year (just before Open Day) the
bike sheds are raided. Rest of the year the school underground meet there.

All pupils – except wimps and swots – automatically
belong to the underground. And that wall is like our news-
paper. Except all the headlines are in a code which no
teacher could ever suss out.

Every piece of graffiti contains a secret known only to the
pupil underground – and now – you. For you are being
given an exclusive, the real low-down on our school. Can
you handle it?

I tell you if you're reading this in a bookshop – go and
buy it right now. Because this book is so brilliant it's
dangerous to read it standing up. You could pass out with
excitement! No fooling.

Before you turn the page – I'm Greg Foord, also called
"Jugger". Everyone reckons my ears stick out. Except me.
Tell you more about me as we go along. (Bet you can't
wait.)

But I want to leap on to the next page now and tell you
about an ancient piece of graffiti which dates back to the 3rd
year. (I'm a 5th year now.) It says STIFF IS UGLY AND
HAS GOT FLEAS.

That's probably the nicest thing ever written about Stiff.
For Stiff was . . . let's jump on to page eight.

Stiff is Ugly and Has Got Fleas

Even before we saw him we hated him.

You would too. How could you not hate someone called Reuben Beardsley. When Byrne, our beloved form teacher, announced that Reuben Beardsley was joining our form there was a riot.

"All right, all right," said Byrne. "His name is not that funny. I hope you'll help him settle in."

Somehow I couldn't imagine anyone called Reuben Beardsley settling into 3B, a form famed for its hard nuts and jokers.

"Nicola, will you go and collect Reuben. He should have arrived in reception now?"

Nicola was the nearest our form had to a wimp. She minced out while Byrne gave us a lecture on the problems of being new. For once everyone was silent, they were busy, trying to picture Reuben Beardsley. Surely he couldn't be as bad as he sounded. He was worse!

Even wimpette Nicola looked ashamed at what she'd hauled in. If Reuben had been a fish you'd have thrown him back in the sea – quickly.

He was a sort of teenage version of the Elephant Man – only not so good-looking. In short – and he was 4' 7" short – Reuben was a pair of mega-thick glasses on a stick. He was immediately christened matchstick man.

Others thought a more appropriate nickname, in view of that greasy tinge his hair always assumed, would be Greaser. Some felt this nickname was too personal and just called him Bender.

But by far the most popular nickname for Reuben and the one I will use, was Stiff. He was called "Stiff" because of the way he moved: all slow and careful and stooped over, like a part of his anatomy was having a massive stiff. It was a nice thought, anyhow.

But looking and walking and sounding like a wally were not enough to make Stiff the most hated boy in the school!

Everything Stiff did lost him marks; minus two marks for those really bad flares, minus two marks for always doing his top button up and another minus point for having collars you could hang-glide (Andy Jones measured Stiff's shirt collar once – 18 inches). Minus four for his haircut (we'd all ask Stiff what size bowl he used). And minus twenty for Stiff's voice. For when Byrne said to Stiff, "I hope you'll be happy here" and Stiff replied, "Thank you very much, Sir" in a haw, haw, "Lick your boots if you like" voice – Stiff was finished.

Farndale School had a major new Public Enemy.

Every day brought news of some fresh atrocity, some additional crime committed by Stiff: Stiff seen talking to a teacher after school and looking as if he was enjoying it; Stiff heard asking a teacher, "If you've already done the homework can you hand it in now?"; Stiff being off games for the fourth week in a row, when we were just dying to carve him up on the football pitch . . .

But we were getting our own back. One band of 4th years carried Stiff into the loos and stuffed his head down the pan to give him a bog-wash. They were going to flush the toilet onto his face, but decided that was too risky. They could really get done for that. Still, they'd given Stiff a warning.

By now, Stiff never even spoke to us. At first he'd asked us where the rooms for lessons were and we always carefully directed him to the wrong room. So then he'd traipsed around the school on his own, drawing himself a beautifully neat map, which we quickly stole.

Yet Stiff was never really alone at Farndale School. We'd all wait for him in the morning and as he'd approach we would all join in one giant chorus of "Stiff! Stiff! Stiff!

Stiff!" singing it really fast and really loud as if Stiff was a football team and we were his supporters. When Stiff left school we'd see him off with another rousing chorus of his name. And throughout the day seven hundred eyes never left Stiff – not for a second.

And then someone had a great idea. Why couldn't Stiff have fleas. After all, his hair always appeared to be caked in grease. And fleas are highly infectious. Probably, if you so much as touched Stiff you'd get fleas too. So began one of the school's most kiddish and popular games, "No returns". Very simple to play.

All you had to do was throw someone – preferably a girl – against Stiff and shout "No returns". Then you couldn't be "got" and the girl had to grab someone else and throw that victim against Stiff – and so on. Stiff was of course the key player. Wherever he was, the game was. Well that was all right, as you got your cheapies too while you dragged a girl across the playground to Stiff's main haunt – the library. (Where else?)

Of course the girl would be hugging and fondling you and just begging you not to throw her against Stiff. If it was a girl you fancied, you'd say, what will you give me if I don't throw you on Stiff. She'd tell you and you'd go away and play a different game.

"No returns" soon spread to not touching anything fouled by the hand of Stiff. If you had to collect books up, you'd refuse to pick up Stiff's. And when you were having your dinner someone would pipe up, "How do you know Stiff didn't use that plate yesterday?" Put you off every time.

Biggest crack was in Science: there were only two long benches – each supposed to seat about fourteen. Only we'd all cram onto one bench while Stiff would sit all by himself on the other.

And while we gave Stiff mighty aggro, what did he do? Nothing. He just sat there taking it. That's what made it worse. I mean, if he'd got mad or even attempted to fight someone, we'd have respected him, maybe even laid off a bit. But he didn't. He'd just lower those big, blank, empty eyes, which didn't have a trace of lad in them – and pour himself into his book.

Once – only once – I remember he showed just the tiniest tremor of anger. He said, "You're not getting to me. You're not."

It was when we'd planted this dirty magazine in Stiff's briefcase. Andy Horne's idea. Then Andy goes over to Stiff, all pretend friendly, and says, "Have you seen my mucky magazine anywhere, mate?"

Stiff did his usual gormo impression and shook his head.

"Thought you might have borrowed it," continued Andy.

Stiff shook and lowered his head.

"Mind if I just check your bag," said Andy sounding like some keen police officer.

Stiff knew it was no use minding – especially as Andy now had a large and appreciative audience. Andy flung all the books out of Stiff's bag, then said dramatically, "Hey folks, look at this." He produced the mucky magazine. "Oh Stiff, you sly sod, what were you doing with it?"

"Didn't know it was there," mumbled Stiff.

"Oh, Stiff, have to do better than that. I'm just going to check you haven't ripped any pages out 'cause I know you."

Andy flicked through the pages. He wasn't a very good actor. We knew Andy had something else planned. Sure enough. "Hello, hello, what's this?"

He pretended to be tugging hard at the pages. "Some of these pages are stuck together, the really juicy pages too. Tell you something else, these aren't stuck with glue." Then, picking up his police impression again, Andy goes, his voice really grave, "Come on now, Stiff, tell the truth, have you been doing something on these pages?"

Laughter rises as everyone, except Stiff, gets the joke. That's when Stiff says, "You're not getting to me, you're not." But even as he says it he starts to slide down his desk, shrinking before our very eyes.

Cruel – certainly. Do I feel ashamed now – sometimes. And yet at the time it didn't seem anything too bad, just a laugh, a way of livening up school.

Anyway, Stiff wasn't human. He was a punch-bag, a safety valve. I mean, Stiff was everything you didn't want to be: he was a short, skinny, greasy, square, posh, swotty, bum-licker. He was also a great comfort.

After all, nobody's perfect. Take me. I'm just 5′ 6″ (and still growing, I hope) only just okay at most sports, got these Mr Spock-style ears and I am going through a Zit phase . . . I used to worry about these defects a lot. But since Stiff I've hardly worried at all. For whatever problems you and I might have, Stiff's got far, far more of them.

None of us guessed how it would end. It ended one Wednesday – never forget it. Strange day all round. Started off when Stiff did a bunk. He'd been in registration and first two lessons. But sometime during break he disappeared. Stiff, swot of the century, skiving. Now there's a sensation.

It seemed too good to be true! We couldn't wait for the teachers to notice but of course they assumed if Stiff was absent he must be sick at home. Their chief collaborator would never do a bunk. And we couldn't grass – not even on Stiff.

But then, just before lunch a new "Stiff" rumour whipped through the school. The source was Gaz. He'd asked to be excused, he was gasping for a fag, and came back almost wetting himself with excitement.

The whispers tore around the classroom. I kept hearing Stiff's name but the rest was muffled.

Then Andy Horne, who was sitting next to me, tried to pass on the news – but he couldn't. He was laughing too much.

"Come on, Horny, spill."

"Sorry, mate, it's just . . ." he started laughing again, then finally, "It's Stiff, he's locked himself in the loo."

12

"Great stuff." I shouted, so loudly I nearly woke up the Geography teacher.

Andy went on, "Gaz noticed one of the loos was locked, knocked on the door to see who was in there and swears he heard Stiff say 'Go away'. Gaz reckons Stiff has been in the loos since break-time."

"Always said Stiff was full of . . ." I didn't need to finish. Andy saw the joke and started passing it on.

By the end of the lesson all of 3B were bubbling with excitement.

"You seem to have really enjoyed that lesson," said the teacher. Silly cow. Like most teachers, she didn't know what went on under her eyes. Didn't want to. Provided we didn't wear white socks and carry trannys about, she didn't care what else we did.

She didn't even notice everyone – girls too – leg it out of her class and make straight for the loos.

The girls hung around outside. A couple did their "Oh poor Stiff" act but they were as excited as we were. We stormed into the loos, led by a proud Gaz. The loo was deserted, as usual. You only used the boys' loo if you were really desperate. I usually hung on.

So we didn't need Gaz to point out which loo Stiff was in. All the loo doors swung open, except one. Locked.

"Stiff, you in there?" called Gaz.

No answer.

"What's the matter, run out of paper," I said.

Laughter and slow, rhythmic chanting, "Stiff Stiff . . ."

One girl, impatient for the next sensation, popped her head round the door. Of course all the blokes went "OOOH, Tania's come to see Stiff's private parts. Pity he hasn't got any", and all that stuff.

But then I shouted, "Shut up a minute and listen." Finally everyone shut up and listened to the weirdest sound ever, Stiff crying.

It was very faint, very feeble, more whimpering than crying.

Reminded me of something. I'd seen this old film about a guy who's buried alive. Then this woman in a big white cape goes out for a midnight stroll and hears this really tiny, but unmistakable wailing coming from a tomb. Thinking it's some trapped animal she leaps off to get help but by the time she's got help the man is really dead. Only thing is, she goes on hearing the wailing, the wailing of the man's ghost.

It spooked her up. And Stiff's crying spooked us up. It wasn't normal somehow. Trust Stiff not to be able even to cry properly.

"Tell Stiff to lay off the cry-baby act," said one lad.

Soon everyone was shouting, "Shut up Stiff", and one group just chanted, "Out, out".

But the wailing went on.

Andy tried to charge the door. Then tried to pretend he hadn't when it wouldn't even budge a centimetre.

The voices continued to yell at Stiff to open up but they were a shade gentler, almost pleading. Everyone was getting restless. This wasn't funny any more.

"Stiff, come out now," ordered a 6th former who'd joined the crowd in the loo.

Next try. "They're all really sorry for what they've done. So open up, Reuben, please." That was from one of the "poor Stiff" splinter group and it was quite a shock hearing someone call Stiff "Reuben".

But Stiff didn't respond. Did he even hear her? Perhaps he had given up listening to us.

"Shall I get a teacher?" whispered Nicola.

A shocking suggestion but Andy, as our unofficial leader, said very quietly, "Go on then, get Byrne."

Then to us he said, "Everyone outside."

We all trooped out. But Stiff's wailing still went right through me – even when I couldn't hear it.

Byrne came and went. He tried everything, reasoning, bullying, begging, but Stiff's tears trickled on. He was sobbing his heart out – very slowly, very painfully.

14

Not even the Headmaster flapping over from his Holy of Holies could get Stiff out. We never actually heard the Headmaster's attempt. We were all sent away and the toilets declared "Out of Bounds". But between lessons we kept a watch.

At 2.30 the Headmaster was outside barking at the teachers toadying around him. At 3.00 the Headmaster was still outside but somebody else had gone in. Couldn't see who. But could guess.

And at 3.35 the toilets were open and ready for business again!

Next day, no Stiff. But I sighted his parents. I knew they were Stiff's parents because they were wearing the same uniform: square trousers, thick glasses, eighteenth-century haircuts. And they were old – sort of antique parents with stooped backs and high quavery yet posh voices.

Heard Daddy Stiff say, "But he's always been such a good boy," then slightly accusingly, "and always had such good reports."

The Head nodded. "My file on him is clean. There's never been any problem with him."

And that was the problem.

A week after his marathon weep-in Stiff returned: just the same, perhaps a little more stooped, a little more elderly.

And as he walked down the corridor to hang up his sturdy, sensible coat, all eyes were on him. Just like before. Only now the teachers had warned us to lay off Stiff and for once I agreed with them. But would everyone else?

Stiff jerked past me. His face as dead as ever. But didn't his hand shake ever so slightly as he placed his coat carefully on the peg. Couldn't be sure. But I did notice how very quietly he moved past us, as if it was the middle of the night and Stiff was anxious not to wake anyone.

Suddenly, from nowhere, Russell Bryant, a major target of piss-taking until Stiff's advent, called out, "Want to borrow a hankie, Stiff?"

15

I was willing Stiff to say something. Bryant was nearly as small as him and doing Bryant over would do wonders for Stiff's image. But Stiff's face remained burnt out. I knew he wouldn't do anything. But someone else did.

Andy Horne leapt forward and picked Bryant up, how you're supposed to pick up puppies. Bryant didn't dare yelp. He just turned a deep red and nodded his head when Andy shouted down his neck, "Leave Reuben alone, all right."

Bryant was released and went scampering away while Andy squared up to Stiff, said, "All right, mate?" and tapped him on the back. First time anyone had dared touch Stiff without saying "No returns" for months.

Then Andy wheeled around on us. "We'll all leave Reuben alone. Okay." Last week Andy was one of Stiff's main tormentors, now he was his champion. Everyone started saying "All right, Reuben?" and "Nice to see you back, mate". Even me. While Stiff, sorry Reuben, seemed to be trying to press his head down into his neck. I think this spectacle of pretend friendship was as painful for him as all the Stiff crap before.

Don't know for sure though. For Reuben barely answered the most palsy-walsy question. Even though for a day or two there was a kind of competition to see who could talk at Reuben the most. You would have thought Reuben was a pet dog: I half expected them to throw sticks for him. This craze, though, was short-lived. The hearty "All right, mates" quickly melted away, a week later Reuben was ignored. No one mocked him, no one spoke to him – you could say Reuben disappeared. There was a flicker of re-interest when Reuben was spotted playing dungeons and dragons with a 2nd year gorm and another flurry when Reuben asked for his YTS scheme to be with the National Trust, but these disturbances quickly faded away, while Reuben went back to his shadow life.

And did I feel sorry for Reuben? Actually I didn't. For in

a funny sort of way I think Reuben finally got what he wanted – he became invisible.

P.S.

All nicknames are a cúrse. A reminder you're not perfect. Like mine. Jugger. Hate that name. Bet Andy hates being Ape (he's really hairy), know Terry Richards hates being called Big Nose . . . but if you get narked the name sticks.

Next story is quite different – just follow me. Over we go to . . .

Denise is the Biggest Slag in Wycombe

"Denise has got cobwebs between her knees," said Phil Scott, one night. And that's pretty strange because Phil Scott is the guy who's been writing DENISE IS THE BIGGEST SLAG IN WYCOMBE all over the school.

What goes on? How can Phil say how easy Denise is – yet at Jo's party – after downing a gallon of cider, complains that Moses couldn't part her knees.

And as for what happened between Denise and Phil later on at Jo's party . . . I don't suss it all. There's only two people who can explain it. But when I asked Phil on Monday he went all quiet and ignored me.

Then I tried Denise. I just said outright, "Why did Phil call you the biggest slag in Wycombe?"

And she goes, "I can't tell you," but adds, "I'll write down why, though, provided you don't censor it."

So here is Denise's uncensored version – which according to her – is the whole truth and nothing but . . .

Why do all blokes pinch my bum? Especially in the art block. And why do blokes think they can touch me up whenever they want? Like it's their right. It used to get me really mad. Not any more. Boys fondle girls, because they think they ought to. It's all to do with image. Proving their manhood. That's all blokes think about, their image.

I tell you, our form's so-called lads, Andy, Gaz and yes, Jugger, are the worst. You should see them walking around school with their hands all dangling down, like they're doing an ape impression. Trouble is, their shoulders roll over too. Cracks me up, every time. But they think it's a hard man's walk.

Only two boys in our year don't pose. Well, one and a half. Don't count Stiff. No, I'm not being nasty. And at least I don't pretend I fancy Stiff, like some girls. The other non-poser, Phil Scott, is very different.

If you live in Bucks you'll know Phil Scott's name. Find it every week on the sports page of the Bucks *Free Press*. Phil breaks about two county records an hour and that's on an off day. Yet, he never boasts or shows off or poses. Doesn't need to, I suppose.

He also rarely attends parties or discos or anything social because he's always training. Bit of a mystery boy really, a mystery boy with big muscles. Now, before we go on I want to make one thing clear. I've never fancied Phil Scott. Never!

He's nice and I like watching him do the high jump but I do not fancy him. Okay!

Anyway, one Saturday afternoon, I was hanging around Hazlemere Crossroads as usual, bored and skint, when along jogs Phil Scott. I gave him a wave and a smile and he came over. He was panting really hard. I assumed this was because he'd been running for a long time. I was wrong.

So we chatted for about a minute. I sensed that he wanted to talk but couldn't think what to say, so I made all the conversation, he just nodded and panted. Then I said, "Well, 'bye then." And he replied all in a rush, "Doing anything special now, Denise?"

"No, just killing time. If I go home I'll be asked to help out so . . ."

He interrupted. "Do you want to come round my house, then. I've got the video of *Purple Rain*." And he looked all eager.

Well, as I said, I was bored, think Prince is magic and I like Phil Scott as a friend, so I went.

I hate it when people write "Little did I know . . ." but honestly it's true. I never guessed what awaited me at Phil Scott's house.

First shock was when Phil's door was opened by his mum saying, "Ah, here she is at last. Thought you two had got lost."

I looked round assuming she was talking to someone behind me. But she wasn't. Yet, how could she expect me . . . We solemnly shook hands. Her lips smiled, her eyes bored into me and she said, "I've heard so much about you, Denise. Would you like a nice cup of tea?"

Resisting a temptation to say, "No, I'd like a nasty one", I just nodded my head. Anything to get rid of her. She scared me.

"Take Denise through to the lounge," she said to Phil. Then she lowered her voice and said all confidingly, "We don't normally use the lounge during the day but as this is rather a special occasion . . ." She gave a false laugh while a grinning Phil led me through a time warp.

The room was cluttered up with chairs Noah had probably sat on and sitting on one of them was someone who looked even older than Noah.

"Grandad, meet Denise."

The old guy creaked to life, stood up and raised his hand as if he were giving a salute. Then I realized I was supposed to shake hands. "He's a good boy, young Philip," he said, gripping my hand. For an old man he had a very firm grip.

"See those cups?" He pointed to a glass shelf staggering under the weight of all the trophies it was carrying. "Won all those and going to win a lot more. He's a lad with a future." And then the Grandad grinned at me, like people do at the end of a commercial. I didn't smile back. No sale. Sorry.

A pot of tea, best china of course, was deposited and Phil's mum began to interview me. Until finally, desperately, I plonked myself on the settee and snapped, "Shall we put the video on, then, Phil?"

Phil's mum fiddled about with a tiny television in the corner of the room and then said, in a voice choking with excitement, "It's all set," like this TV was about to beam pictures from space.

Thankfully, Phil's mum went back to the crypt while Phil and I sat on opposite ends of the couch and Grandad, pretended to be dozing in his corner. But I decided to blot this peculiar family out and let Prince take over. Even on a screen the size of a postage stamp, Prince was brilliant. I sat back and tried to enjoy the show but I couldn't. For I was being watched.

Phil wasn't looking at the video, he was looking at me looking at the video. And every time my eyes caught his, he'd give me this really lopsided smile. There was no getting away from it – Phil fancied me.

I never imagined Phil fancying anyone, certainly not me. Yonks ago, Jo (my sometime best friend) told me she'd seen Phil giving me the eye. But she reckons everyone gives me the eye, does it to annoy me.

Half-way through *Purple Rain* I spotted Phil's grandad having a fit. He was waving his hands about in the air like he was directing imaginary traffic. Was he doing his exercises or freaking out to Prince? But I soon realized what old Gramps was up to. He was directing Phil to . . . a hand glided across my back and landed on my wrist. To be exact, it landed on my gold chain, the one I'd bought in Paris. Then this hand started rubbing the chain up and down my wrist.

"What are you doing?" I whispered. "Happy?" he murmured, tapping my hand.

I took my hand away. "Yeah, really good film," and I fixed my gaze onto Prince.

When the second the film finished I shot up. "Thanks a lot, must go."

Before I left I had to shake hands with Grandad, have a second interview with Phil's mum and then Phil and I were tactfully left alone in the hallway.

His hand went round me. It was like being held by a vice.

Then more heavy breathing as Phil tried to kiss me. Throughout the kiss, Phil kept his mouth closed and pressed hard, it was like being kissed by a hoover.

Close up, I noticed all these black dots which covered his face. I wondered if he ever joined them all up. Then he said, "What do you want to do tonight?"

"Tied up tonight. Babysitting."

"Want me to come along?"

"Better not."

"I'll walk you home then."

Now I was breathing heavily. "No, no, honestly."

"It's no trouble."

"It's okay. Must go."

He patted me on the back. "Denise, I was just wondering, when you love someone do you look into their face or their eyes?"

I ran all the way home. Talk about risky.

At last I was safe. But as I opened the door the phone was ringing. "It's for you," said Mum.

Yes, it was him, just checking I'd got back all right and to let me know that if I changed my mind and wanted him to babysit he still could.

Four more phone calls on Sunday. ("Are you busy all day?") And Monday morning 8.30, guess who was waiting at the corner shops for me.

Normally Jo meets me there but this morning, "Jo had to go on," he said displaying his special gormo grin, "so I'll accompany you if you don't mind."

"Oh no."

Just before we reached school, he suddenly plunged his hand into his bag and produced a massive teddy bear. "This is for you," he said.

It was very large, very yellow and very embarrassing.

Of course everyone saw me walk into school with Phil Scott and teddy bear. All the girls went "Aaah" when they saw the teddy bear and "Oooh" when Phil indicated he had bought the bear for me.

More "Aaahs" when Phil presented me at break-time with a large, soppy card on which he had written, MY HEART IS YEARNING FOR YOU.

By the end of the day all the 5th year assumed Phil and I were going steady. Clearly, Phil did too. I was the only dissenter. Action, quick action, was demanded. I must tell Phil I don't fancy him. But I hate, absolutely hate doing things like that.

I used to get Jo to inform my boyfriends when they were chucked. Until one bloke told me what really upset him was not me chucking him – but someone he hardly knew screaming out, "Denise is chucking you" right in the middle of a disco. (Jo's got no tact – and she's a closet-shy person.)

So after that I did all my own chucking. But how do you chuck someone you're not even going out with, if you see what I mean.

That night, I wrote Phil four letters, tore them all up. If I rang him I'd probably get his weird mother on the line, there was nothing else for it, I must tell him face to face.

Next morning face to face at 8.30, but I couldn't tell him then, too knackering first thing. Instead, I asked if I could see him after school. He replied that he was tied up every night after school with training, although if I wanted him to miss training of course he would. Then I suggested lunchtime. But where? Jo and I have all our private chats in the girls' loo, but I couldn't invite Phil in there. Nothing else for it – the Mound.

The Mound lies at the back of the back field and is where couples go to do their coupling. No wonder Phil was panting. Bet he spent the whole of morning school panting. He obviously thought he was in for a session of torrid love and instead . . .

If only I fancied him. Why didn't I fancy him? He wasn't bad-looking – especially in his P.E. kit. He was kind, generous, almost too eager to please. Okay, he had a dappy family but who hasn't. No, Phil passed all my tests, except one. The most important one.

How can I describe it? Well, have you ever gone to sleep on a really warm night with tons of blankets and sheets covering you and when you wake up you feel so hot you can hardly breathe. It's agony. And those are also the symptoms of deep fancying. Like there was this really hunky guy I met on holiday, tall, dark and ginger, I just had to see him for my body temperature to jump to boiling point.

I tell you, when I'm turned on it's like I'm wearing a life-sized electric blanket – on maximum. I get so hot and sticky and choked up, it's marvellous. But Phil, sorry he didn't even turn on one small radiator. Nothing. That's when I knew I had to be cruel to be kind. However difficult. Even though when I saw him bounding towards me I knew his little heart was turning cartwheels, and he was probably so hot his skin was peeling.

Phil jumped down behind the Mound, said, "Hello, Denise," and gave me a very thin, very comfortable hug.

Having got that over I dived in. "Phil I want to say something. I really like you." A broad grin grew on his face . . . "as a friend." The broad grin disappeared.

"I hope we'll always be friends. And I know people say ' Just friends ' but actually no one or hardly anyone goes out with anyone for long . . . but you keep your friends for years and years."

He nodded, going "Uhuh" but not saying anything else. Then I looked at his eyes – very blue his eyes – and they told me his heart had stopped. I finished quickly. "So thanks for the teddy bear. It's really nice, a very sweet thought. But don't give me any more – presents."

He stood up. "Better go," he said and sprinted away while I spent the rest of the lunch-time behind the Mound, thinking why is life so messy. Why couldn't God arrange it so that we only fancied people who fancied us.

However, I had to put the mix-up with Phil behind me. It

wasn't my fault, sad though it was. Next day I succeeded. A new horrible event totally overshadowed it. Sprawled all over the wall known as the smokers' wall was – DENISE IS THE BIGGEST SLAG IN WYCOMBE. Gave me a real shock I can tell you. The letters were so huge, so unmissable, so vicious.

Couldn't mean me, though, could they? I tried to think of other Denises who could be called "slags". I couldn't think of any. Back in the classroom I saw on my desk – DENISE IS THE BIGGEST SLEASE BAG IN WYCOMBE. Soon, wherever I went I saw this vile graffiti. Bet if I went in the Head's Office I'd find it there too. I now knew I was the Denise referred to.

But who would write such horrible things about me? Clearly this wasn't a joke. Someone hated my guts. And I assumed it was a girl. Which one? I hadn't stolen anyone's boyfriend recently.

I asked Jo about the graffiti and she pretended she hadn't seen it. That's when I knew every girl in the 5th year was discussing it with every other 5th-year girl – except me.

Tell you something else, I bet Jo knows who's writing DENISE IS THE BIGGEST SLAG IN WYCOMBE. So on Friday after school and after two days of seeing my name plastered everywhere, I said to Jo, "Level with me, Jo, who's been writing all that nasty stuff about me."

"What stuff?"

"You know – DENISE IS THE BIGGEST SLAG IN WYCOMBE. It's all over the school."

"Oh yes, I have seen it," said Jo, colouring a little.

"You couldn't fail to see it – but who's been writing it?"

"You know," said Jo quickly.

"No I don't."

"You must."

"Honestly, I don't know."

Jo paused, "It's to do with your ex."

"What, Jimmy Pearce?"

Jo turned on me. "Are you trying to be funny? You know, I mean, Phil Scott."

Even then I didn't realize. "You mean some girl is getting at me because of Phil Scott."

"No, Denny, I mean Phil Scott is writing the stuff himself. You must have guessed that."

But when Jo saw my face she knew I hadn't guessed . . . not for a second. Why would a decent, gentle, sports hero like Phil Scott spread such vicious lies?

Unfortunately, Jo interpreted my shock as meaning I was pining away for Phil Scott. She goes, "It's hard being chucked by a guy you really care for."

"Phil didn't finish it," I said sharply.

"You're not saying you finished it." Jo sounded amazed.

"No, I didn't finish it because we never started."

"Oh, come off it, Denny, the whole school knows you're mad about Phil Scott."

"What!"

She linked my arm. "We all know what you're going through."

I unlinked my arm. This was like one of those nightmares which keep getting worse and worse.

"Listen, Jo, have I ever told you I'm madly in love with Phil Scott?"

"No." She paused. "But Phil Scott has."

I stopped walking and stood right in front of her. She stepped backwards. "I'm not moving another yard and neither are you until you tell me exactly what Phil Scott has been saying about me." I added, "Please."

Jo told me. In fact I think she quite enjoyed telling me.

"Phil Scott is saying that you invited yourself round his house on Saturday afternoon, tried to get off with him, kept ringing and ringing him and on Sunday you and he . . . did it."

"Dream on," I murmured trying to hide my anger.

Joe continued. "According to Phil you're obsessed with sex and on Monday – despite him giving you a present and a card – you got off with someone else. That's why on Tuesday he said he was chucking you, you were just too easy – and made him look a fool."

"That sly, miserable . . ." I lapsed into swearing while Jo watched me anxiously. Then I turned on her. "Why didn't you tell me all this before?"

"I . . . er."

"You thought what that rat said might be true, didn't you?"

"No, not exactly. I mean, any other bloke I wouldn't even listen to, but Phil Scott, he's not like the others."

"No, he's worse. Spreading lies about me just to make himself look good. Fancy saying we went all the way together. Why he can't even kiss properly."

"So you have kissed him, then," said Jo quickly.

"Once – never again. He, also following instructions from his grandfather, did actually fondle my gold chain. And that's all our bodily contact. The rest of the time I spent telling his mother how many 'O' levels I'm sitting. Have you seen his mother?"

"Yeah, very protective. Since his dad died she calls Phil the man of the house, makes him check all the doors every night."

"Didn't know his father was dead."

"Heart attack."

"Anyway, I'm sure that's very sad but no excuse for what he's done to me. I'm going round his house now to give him a right earful."

"I've got a better idea," said Jo. She spoke slowly. "Phil Scott is coming to my party tonight."

"Phil Scott going to a party?"

"Yeah, I was pretty amazed. So why don't you have it out with him there."

I thought of Phil's house and that ghastly mother

wandering in and out with tea and questions. "Jo, I hate to ruin your party and all, but that punk isn't going to know what's hit him tonight."

Jo stared at me, drinking in my anger. "You're really uptight about this, aren't you? Can't blame you."

We linked arms again. "But don't worry about my party, a big row often makes a party." Then, in case she sounded too excited, she added, "And I'll do anything to help you get back your good name."

I arrived at the party late. I'd gone home so wound up I had a row with my mum and nearly wasn't allowed out at all.

Jo met me at the door. My greeting. "Where is he?"

Jo's eyes were shining. "Denny, something's happened."

"Go on."

"Well, Phil was the first guest to arrive – he was here before seven o'clock. He drank and drank, mixed his drinks and now . . ."

I interrupted. "He's lying upstairs, out of his head."

"No, he's outside pretending to be a dolphin."

"What!"

"He suddenly stripped off all his clothes – except for his pants – and ran out into the garden to do his dolphin impression. He's doing it now."

"This, I must see," I said.

I joined about half the party outside. They were standing round in a semi-circle, clapping and laughing while Phil Scott capered across the garden, making swimming motions with his hands. Then he called out, "Now my dolphin impression," and goes "Click, click, click, click. That is the noise of a very thirsty dolphin," he looked round, "a very thirsty dolphin, click, click, click."

"He wants a drink," shouted someone.

A beer can was thrown at him which he caught easily.

"You didn't know dolphins could drink beer did you?" he said, pouring most of the beer down his chest. Then he started clapping his hands together going, "Aaarp, Aaarp, Aaarp, Aaarp – this is the sound of a very sexy dolphin."

Some people found this hysterical – a few were crying on the floor with laughter. I also felt like crying – but not with laughter. How could he make such a spectacle of himself.

He was now gambolling around the garden calling, "I'm looking for a seal. Aaarp, Aaarp," and sniffing at the girls.

I should have enjoyed seeing him degrade himself. But I didn't. I stared at his strong shoulders, lean muscular body. Hours and hours of training had helped make him look so impressive. Blokes often spoke about their "tool". Phil's whole body was his "tool" which he had built up and was now destroying.

Suddenly, I shouted out, "Phil Scott, stop behaving like a wally."

At a stroke the laughter stopped, the dolphin impression stopped, silence. I almost enjoyed the dramatic impact I was making.

Everyone assumed Phil and I were Hazlemere's answer to Romeo and Juliet – so the crowd parted to let me through.

Then I shouted, "Why did you write all those lies about me."

"They're no lies," he yelled back, "they're all true."

"They're lies," I screamed.

"They're true – you are a slag."

Clearly this shouting match was not doing my image any good. So I snarled, "I'll talk to you inside."

"Use my bedroom if you like," said Jo. She turned to Phil, "If that's all right with you."

"Yeah, I'll just swim in," he said and started making breast stroke motions. He really was pissed.

The crowd followed us in, no doubt disappointed that the next scene was taking place off stage.

I arrived in the bedroom first. Then Phil staggered into view, a beer can in his hand.

"Close the door," I said. He obeyed. "Now we're alone,"

I continued, "tell me why you've been writing all those lies about me."

"You messed me about." He spat the words at me, like he was now impersonating a very angry dolphin. "You're a user, just using me to get presents out of me."

"Crap. It's only you haven't been out with many girls – and don't know that a girl can go round to a bloke's house as a friend. And that's what I did. But you'd obviously planned the whole thing – and told your family I was your future wife or something." I paused. He was standing in front of me still wearing only his underpants. He looked very young, very alive.

"I'm just going to open a window," I said. "It's getting a bit stuffy in here."

I can never open windows. They always seem to jam in my hands. This one was no exception. I pushed all my weight against it. Couldn't budge it. Then Phil just seemed to run his finger-nail against it; opened instantly.

His fingers touched mine. I tried to get a gulp of fresh air but instead I got a mouthful of Phil Scott. He grabbed me and pressed his lips so roughly against mine I was certain they'd start bleeding. Then his tongue tore into my mouth – no holding back this time. I must fight him off – in a minute.

For the first time Phil frightened me. He was almost naked and I could feel his body tight against mine, desperately forcing himself onto me. And it was so hot I could hardly breathe. I pushed him away.

"Open the windows," I murmured.

"They're open," he said.

"Can't be."

He lunged for me again. He was shaking with excitement and passion.

"No, no," I said. The heat was making me dizzy. I swayed towards the window and gulped in gallons of fresh air. Then I turned on him. "How dare you try to get off

30

with me. You don't know the first thing about girls — grabbing me like that."

He didn't answer, just stood there shivering. I staggered to the door. I was baking. "I'm going home now and I'd like you to know you've ruined this week and this party for me — and I don't want to speak to you again, ever."

I slammed the door and just stood on the outside, my head throbbing, my mind reeling, my heart . . .

I pushed open the door again.

He was sitting on the bed, his head in his hands.

"And another thing . . ."

He looked up.

"Ring me tomorrow night," I said.

P.S.

Was going to stick a picture of myself in the book. Not for a pose — just because I thought you might like to know what I look like. But I couldn't find a decent photo.

There's loads of me when I was about seven. People used to say I should be in adverts. I was so cute-looking. I'm still cute, today — I'm a blond hair, blue eyes, cheeky smile job.

I'm not showing off — not much — just thought you'd like to know. Anyway, come and meet Bogie — been writing the story all night. Think you'll find it a crack.

Bogie's Sticky One

April 7th – Period 4

We hadn't intended to bring about a killing. Not at all. I mean, you push every teacher as far as you can. You've got to. That's how you suss out how far you can go.

But with Bogie, there were no limits. You just went on pushing him and pushing him. And every day a new and better Bogie wobbly: like yesterday when we let those frogs out onto his desk. Of course, Bogie ran after them, banging into all the desks and yelling his head off. Whilst particles of angry gob swamped his beard.

Or last week when we nicked the keys to Bogie's stock cupboard and locked him inside. He ran against the door like a mad bull, "Let me out! Let me out!" Then suddenly he says all quietly, "If you open the door now we'll forget the whole thing."

Of course we opened up. We were fond of Bogie. And occasionally, just occasionally, we'd let Bogie win. We'd pretend his shouting fit had scared us rigid. Made the next round all the more exciting. And we quickly became experts at teasing him, baiting him, sending him crazy. Until one day we went too far.

Never forget the date – APRIL 7th, PERIOD 4. A special date. Been planning it for weeks. We even wrote about it on the wall. BOGIE'S STICKY ONE APRIL 7th PERIOD 4. All the underground knew. But none of the teachers even guessed that we were planning a one-period strike – just for Bogie.

No books, no work, no hands up, no nothing. Not very

different from a normal Bogie lesson. Except today, we wouldn't even pretend to work. Unanimous too. (Stiff was, unsurprisingly, away.) Worried about Nicola, though. She sat squirming nervously in the front. Must keep an eye on her.

Then Gaz, our lookout, goes "Bogie". Immediately we started shouting and talking loudly. Wanted the lesson to sound normal. Bogie worked through his scales: "There must be silence now. I mean that – come on. Come on, settle down now. I don't want any more noise," ending with a screeching, "Be quiet." Bogie was already hoarse.

Of course, Bogie wore this really disgusting green jacket – hence his nickname. As usual, the jacket was decorated with flicked ink. Bogie jumped on to a temporary lull in the noise to say, "Right, *Lord of the Flies* books out please." He was trying a new trick on us, deliberately speaking really quietly. Idea was, we would strain our ears to hear him. Instead, everyone called out "What", "Pardon", "Can't hear you".

"Get your books out," screamed Bogie in his normal voice.

"No need to shout," said Andy.

"Well come on, then, books out."

No one moved.

"What's the matter, are you all deaf? Your mothers want to wash your ears out in the morning."

"Calling me dirty?" says Andy.

"No, I'm not. Although I think some of you could take more care over your appearance."

"Who? Who? Come on, name someone," yelled Andy.

"You mean me, don't you?" said Denise and she pretended to cry.

Jo got out of her seat. "Don't cry, Denise," she said. "I'm sure sir didn't mean to say you were dirty," cooed Jo.

"Josephine, get back to your seat," said Bogie.

"But she's crying," said Jo.

Denise obligingly raised the level of her crying.

"Now come on, Denise," said Bogie. "Stop this nonsense. And the rest of you, come along now, books out. We're already very behind."

Once again no one stirred.

Bogie started panicking. "What is the matter with you all this morning?" Then he tried a typical teacher trick. Isolate. "Rubi, books out, please."

Rubi, a quiet pretty girl with swottish tendencies, shook her head. "No."

"What do you mean 'No'." By now his beard was receiving a thorough watering. "Rubi – get your *Lord of the Flies* book out."

"Sorry, can't," she said, shaking her head.

Bogie stared at his class. Never had it been so quiet. That really freaked him up. Desperately he made for the weak link – our wimpette. "Nicola, will you get your book out, please?"

Tension rose. If Nicola blacklegged, a few other girls might too.

I placed the paper in my mouth. Then chewed carefully. Had to get just the right texture. Be quick too. Nicola might well need a reminder of the dangers of blacklegging.

But even without my reminder Nicola said, "I cannot get any book out. We're on strike."

"What!" Bogie was boiling up nicely. Then he yelled, "Nicola get your book out." It wasn't an order – it was a plea. He was begging her.

Nicola's hand twitched violently. Then it lowered itself down towards her bag. She was weakening. Action was needed. I swiftly removed the paper from my mouth. Just right. Had a nice pulp to it. Bogie had both his hands on Nicola's desk. His face was almost level with hers. Was she staring into Bogie's eyes. Impossible. Bogie didn't have any eyes. Just deep dark recesses under his eyebrows. But he was frightening Nicola. Her hand was definitely in her bag.

I placed the paper on my ruler. Gave it a swift but expert flick. I really had intended to hit Nicola but seeing Bogie's face so close, so tempting . . . I scored a bull's-eye. Bogie jerked up and started rubbing his forehead. He looked confused. While Nicola sat up, hands firmly placed on the desk. Mission accomplished. The class was in uproar now until Andy raised his hand. He didn't want any teachers coming in. That would ruin everything.

"Who did that?" said Bogie, when Andy had quietened the class.

"I did."

He stared at me, stroking his cheek. Then he opened his mouth really wide, as if he was about to sing an opera. "Well just come out here."

"Can't, sir."

"I beg your pardon, young man."

"And I beg yours – but I can't come out. Not allowed to. We're only allowed to sit behind desks. Why, walking up to you would be like crossing a picket line."

The best teachers, like the best card players, never give anything away. You never know when you've got them. But Bogie showed his hand right away. No aces, just anger, frustration and terror. "But you can't go on strike," he cried.

"Unanimous. Lightning strike," I said.

Bogie tried to reason with me. "Now look here, Foord, you're not a complete idiot."

"I'll try harder."

"Doing something like this could be very dangerous for you." He paused, then said as dramatically as he could, "You might get expelled."

"Thank you, sir."

Andy cut in. "You'd have to expel the whole class, sir." Then Andy made a slight signal. Bogie missed it. No one else did. Immediately, Edward and James went into their imaginary balls routine. They pretended to pass round this ball, throwing it all over the class. And it sent Bogie crazy every time. Like now. "Right, I'll have that."

"What?" goes Edward.

"That ball. I'll have that. There are no balls allowed in my classroom."

This line, of course, got a lot of laughs and distracted Bogie's attention away from . . . The desks were slowly but surely moving around him. The three rows were becoming a circle. Soon Bogie would be surrounded.

"I'll put my balls away now, sir," said Edward.

"Thank you," said Bogie. "And perhaps we can get on with some work. *Lord of the Flies* books out. I'm setting an essay. Trace the descent into savagery . . . Well come on, write this down! Come on!" Solidarity stared Bogie in the face. Panicking now, he shouted. "All right! All right! I'm not having this, Greg Foord, out."

"Why me?" I said, all pretend indignant.

"Because you threw a missile at me."

"A missile. It was only a bit of gobbed-up paper." Laughter and Bogie squeaking, "How dare you! How dare you! Haven't your parents taught you anything? Or are they as ignorant as you?"

"Leave my parents alone," I said, actually getting a bit annoyed.

"In all my years of teaching I've never encountered such rudeness. And I've been teaching for over twenty years," said Bogie.

Still stung by his comment, about my parents, I taunted, "Perhaps it's time you retired, then."

After that, Bogie clenched his teeth like a vicious dog and snarled, "Get out! Get out!" He kept saying it over and over, his voice going all high-pitched, "Get out! Get out!"

This is what we wanted. Everyone cheered. Bogie screeched. "I'm not saying it again."

"Yes, you are," shouted someone.

"Foord, get out," Bogie gasped.

"But why, sir?"

"Why! Why!" cried Bogie. "Because you're not working, that's why."

"But, sir, no one's working so everyone should be sent out," I replied. Roars of agreement.

Andy shouted, "Come on, lads, everybody out."

Andy had forgotten all about keeping the noise down now. He was too excited; we all were. So when Andy stood up and pretended to leave, we all copied him.

"Will you all sit down," said Bogie.

"But you told us to leave," said Andy.

"Yeah, make up your mind," shouted Gaz.

"All right, all right," said Bogie and he ran behind his desk. He sat there, clenching his desk really hard, as if he was preventing it from taking off. We watched him, fascinated. Then, having steadied himself, he carefully opened his black briefcase. Bogie never knew what he'd find in his briefcase. Today a butterfly shot out. Class before had put it there.

We all pretended to try to catch it until Bogie called out. "All right, all right, from now on I'm writing down the names of anyone who does not work. From now on. So the joke is over – book out."

Again the classroom was suddenly hushed, quiet, expectant. Suddenly, Bogie pounces on Nicola. "Young lady, I've asked you to get your book out."

"Why are you picking on Nicola?" shouted Gaz.

"Yeah, picks on Jugger, now Nicola."

Nicola looked scared. But she didn't move.

"Now Nicola, I'm giving you one more chance, get your book out immediately. Come on," he added.

Nicola shook her head, staring at the floor.

"Well, I'm very much afraid, Nicola, I'm going to have to write your name down in my book."

"Want her phone number too?" called out Jo.

"Dirty old man," said someone else.

Bogie did his best to sound frightening. "So, Nicola, your name goes down in my book for detention this Thursday."

"Oooh!" from the class while Nicola looked as if she was going to cry. Her first ever detention.

Bogie then advanced on the next weak link: Rubi. "Rubi, book open, please." Bogie tried to sound brisk, in command. Rubi did a massive beamer but nothing else.

Bogie reverted to his whispering act again. "Then I'm afraid, Rubi, your name is also going down on my detention list."

"Turn the volume up," yelled Gaz.

Bogie carried on whispering. He could see he was getting to Rubi. Bogie moved his hand across to his detention book then said softly, "So, come on, Rubi, open your text."

You know, I think Rubi might well have led the strike-breaking, if Andy hadn't called out, "Wanker, Wanker."

Bogie blew up. "How dare you call me that. How dare you. You didn't realize I'd know what that means. Well, I do know."

Everyone picked up on this. "Tell us what it means, sir. Go on."

I called, "Please, sir, tell me what a wanker is. I want to know."

"Don't be even sillier than you are, Foord," said Bogie.

"But, sir, please tell me, I want to increase my vocabulary."

"Yeah, go on, sir," urged the class.

"Right, that's it. Foord, detention."

In my well-practised indignant voice – "But why, sir? I only asked you what a word meant. Thought that was the point of English, to improve your vocabulary and now I'm getting a detention for wanting to learn."

"Any more from you, Foord, and it will be a double."

Everyone pretended to be worked up although a Bogie detention was an even bigger crack than his lessons.

"Rubi, will you go and get Mr Bryne," said Bogie. He was playing his last card – getting another teacher.

"No, sir, I won't," said Rubi, quite boldly now.

"How dare you! How dare you!" cried Bogie. "In all my years I've never met a class like this. Right, there's nothing for it. I'm going to get the Headmaster."

"Oooh, not really," we shouted.

"Yes, that's it," said Bogie. He jumped up from his desk and tried to get out. But every way he turned was barricaded with desks. Bogie was trapped. He jumped up and down like an over-wound clockwork toy. Then he faced us, yelling, "Move the desks! Move the desks!" His head shook continuously, covering his shoulders in dandruff. "Move these desks back."

Normally we would have ended the joke there. However, now we'd tasted blood. Couldn't stop if we wanted to. We were as worked up and frenzied as Bogie.

"Move the desks," cried Bogie again. His head was shaking so violently you wouldn't have been surprised if it had dropped off. Like Vyvyan's head in *The Young Ones*. In fact this lesson was becoming just like a *Young Ones* sketch. You felt anything could happen.

The next happening was the wildest yet. Bogie suddenly dropped down on to all fours. We all started making barking noises calling out, "Good boy, Bogie", "Here Bogie", and rubbing our shoes on his back while he was crawling under the desks by the door. Then he stood up, his jacket now decorated with a variety of footprints and mud. "I'm going to get the Head," he snarled to the door handle as he charged out.

"What about that, then," said Andy.

We all just nodded, dazed. It was the sort of lesson you dream about.

"But if he brings the Head back," said Nicola suddenly.

"Well, we're all in it." A few girls agreed.

"Don't think he will," said Andy, so confidently we all stared at him. "You see, just before the lesson I had a look in the staff car park and Moggie's (Headmaster's nickname from Morgan) car wasn't there. Reckon he's out all morning."

"But what if Moggie is back?" said Nicola.

Andy stood up. "I bet Bogie hasn't gone anywhere near the Head's office, anyway. Come on lads, let's see."

About half a dozen of us jostled out of the door, then Andy goes, "Shut up, you lot." For at the top of the corridor, standing in front of a noticeboard was Bogie.

"Told you he wouldn't get very far," whispered Andy.

"What a nut-job," said Gaz.

"Ssh. Don't let Bogie see us. Then we can rip the piss out of him," said Andy.

We crept back to the classroom, passed on the news, quietened down the laughing and awaited Bogie's return.

Finally, a breathless Bogie opened the door and said in a solemn, war-has-been-declared voice, "I've just spoken to the Head."

Andy signalled everyone not to laugh – yet. Then he asked, all mock-serious, "What did the Head say?"

"He said he was shocked to hear of your behaviour and he wanted to see all the pupils involved in this so-called strike."

"When?" asked Denise.

"Now," said Bogie.

Andy drew his bluff. "All right then, lads, there's nothing for it." He stood up. "Let's go." We all stood up while Bogie cowered by the door. "Where are you all going?" he screeched. "To see the Head like you said," replied Andy.

"Now – er, just wait a minute," blustered Bogie. "The Head also said if you call off this silly strike now, right now, he'd forget the whole thing."

"Really," said Andy.

"Yes," said Bogie eagerly.

Andy pretended to consider this. Poor Bogie really thought he had us. You could see his hopes rising.

Then Andy goes, "No, sorry and all that, but a strike is a strike. We can't break it. We'll go and give ourselves up to the Head – come on."

We poured out of our seats and all stood before Bogie.

"Go back to your seats," squeaked Bogie.

And we saw on his face something you should never see on any teacher's face – terror. And the more terrified Bogie looked, the more stirred up we became. Never before had we realized how powerful we could be. Just seeing Bogie squirming about by the door made me feel quite drunk.

"Bogie! Bogie!" called out Terry, one of the quieter boys who would never have dared call Bogie by his nickname before. "Bogie! Bogie!" chanted the class. Some, remembering his crawling under the desks on all fours, started going, "Here boy. Here Bogie."

Everyone, even Nicola, was calling things out. No one knew what was going to happen next. It was like in those cartoons where a character falls off a cliff but instead of tumbling to the ground starts walking on air. That's what we were doing.

Then, suddenly, Bogie stopped reacting. He just stood there, his head bowed, his shoulders hunched, his whole body sagging. He seemed to be ageing before our eyes. Then he turned his back on us, turned the door handle and disappeared. We stood there, blinking, as if the lights had gone up suddenly in the middle of a film.

Then Andy shouts, "After him lads." Gaz and I followed Andy. So did Denise and Jo.

Last time we followed Bogie we'd been really high. This time we were apprehensive, wary, not laughing any more. We trailed Bogie down the corridor, assuming he was going towards the staff room (and the Head's office). Instead he was staggering towards the car park. We had to follow Bogie at a snail's pace so that we didn't catch him up. Bogie moved like some elderly athlete, until he reached the car park. Then he appeared to rejuvenate himself. Springing into his car and revving it up as if he was about to break a speed record.

We waved and shouted to him. He saw us. He waved back. Really friendly. Then he tried to run us over. Car missed us by inches. It actually grazed Gaz who toppled over. "Did you see that?" he yelled. "Bloody maniac."

"I don't think he knows what he's doing," said Jo.

We watched Bogie circle round the car park again. Then we automatically darted out of the way as he came near us. Jo jumped into the hedge, she was so frightened. As he passed us, he waved and I caught a glimpse of his face. Never forget it. He looked like his brain had gone on holiday. Totally mad. Then he disappeared. "Poor Bogie's really flipped," I said.

"I don't think so," Gaz said. "I think for the first time Bogie knew exactly what he was doing. He was trying to brick us up as a repayment for all the times we bricked him up."

"No," I argued. "Didn't you see that weird look on his face. He was totally out of control, hadn't a clue what he was doing."

"Anyway," said Denise. "He's gone – thanks to us."

"Be back in five minutes," said Andy.

"No," said Jo, "he's run away, that's what Bogie's done. Can't blame him, either, after all we did to him."

"You can talk," said Andy, "You were in there, messing him about like everyone else."

"I know, I'm not saying anything, just I think we went too far."

"It was his fault, though," said Denise. "If a teacher can't keep order he shouldn't be a teacher."

Andy interrupted the debate. "Better go back and tell the others what's happened." As soon as we entered – there was silence. There were some giggles when we told them about Bogie's retreat. But not many. Mostly people looked like they had a bad hangover. No one had expected – or wanted – Bogie actually to leave.

"Do you think we should get a teacher?" said Nicola.

She was immediately shouted down. Still, no one quite

knew what to do. And in the end the problem was solved for us. Mr Lascelles, the Head of Upper School, had become suspicious of the quiet in Bogie's room. While he was interrogating us, a caretaker arrived with an eye-witness account of Bogie in the car park . . .

Next day, a supply teacher, the first of many. All useless – but none in Bogie's league.

And a lecture from the Head. Moggie, famed for his sarky comments and bad breath, went for the jugular. "I hope no one in this miserable class is feeling pleased with themselves. Mr Williams was an M.A. from Cambridge, he could have taught you much. But he made one error. He didn't realize that schoolchildren are a hybrid. For those of you who don't know what a hybrid is, I'll tell you—" he smiled, an undertaker's smile. "It means a mixture. Schoolchildren are a mixture of human and animal. In your case, mostly animal. And I know how to treat animals." That smile again before his parting words, "You've lost a fine teacher and I hope you all feel guilty."

I felt sorry for Bogie – but not guilty. We're one side, teachers the other, the winning side. For teachers hold all the ammunition. So can you blame us for going crazy when we have a teacher who can only fire blanks – and usually in the wrong direction.

We never saw Bogie again. And we were very sorry about that. We enjoyed pushing Bogie. Naturally. But we hadn't intended to bring about a killing. Honestly!

P.S.

Here are some exclusive, juicy quotes from my latest school report. Can you top these: *Geography*: Gregory (!!) has achieved his goal and gained almost 0% in his examinations. (That Geography teacher hates me, as you may have guessed. I've given him plenty of jip.) *History*: Greg didn't deserve his examination result but he is obviously capable.

(See, even when I get a good exam mark they criticize.)
Maths: No effort but no trouble. (That's the most insulting, I think.)

Now there's my form teacher's summing up: "Gregory makes a maximum of effort outside the classroom and a minimum within it."

Dad read that comment twice and says to me, "What's he on about?"

I said, "I think he means I do my best work in the corridors."

But I did get one decent comment (allowed one, aren't you!) for *English*: I am very encouraged by Greg's progress. He is a most talented young man.

Think Dad thought I'd forged that entry. But no – it came from a pretty special teacher. Total opposite to Bogie. We call him C.K.

Story starts as we meet him for the first time.

C.K. Rules, OK

"He hasn't got a wooden leg," said Gaz.

"And yet his legs are so skinny. No one has legs four inches wide," I said. But apparently he did. It was very disappointing.

Still, what do you expect from a new teacher who's young and male. Teaching is just a job for old people who enjoy moaning. So when a young guy becomes a teacher there's something very wrong. Is he bent? Is he a gorm? Who could spot his defects first?

The new teacher walked in, smiling.

"He's gay," said Andy confidently.

"Hi, everyone, my name is Chris Kenting." Trendy suit (for a teacher), grey leather tie, white socks, big smile. We were suspicious, very suspicious. "I'd like everyone to call me Chris," he continued. "I hate all the sir nonsense."

We started firing questions at him, just for the novelty of calling him Chris. Then we went back to calling him sir. Wasn't natural calling a teacher by his Christian name. Made a teacher sound too human. Later on we compromised, called him C.K. – his initials.

"Right," said C.K. "I'm going to discover how talented you all are. Thought we'd start with a poem." Groans all round.

"Can't do poetry," said Gaz.

"Rubbish, everyone can do poetry. I'm sure you've all written a poem which begins 'There was a . . .'"

"You mean we can write dirty poems," said Andy.

"You can write anything you like," said C.K.

"Has it got to rhyme?" asked Denise.

"No."

"How long has it got to be?"

"As long as you like. Look, there are no rules. Just write what you want – and enjoy yourself."

"Reckon," murmured Gaz.

"Let's give this jerk some poems to remember," said Andy to Gaz and me. Of course, we were on the back row.

As we wrote we kept cracking up. "Listen to this," said Andy. "John and Mary from the dairy. John pulled out his long and hairy. Mary said Cor . . ."

"You can't write that," interrupted Denise who was sitting in front of us.

"Why not?" said Andy. "We were told to write anything we wanted."

"He'll send you to the Head," said Denise.

"That's it," I cried. "I'll write a poem about Moggie."

We kept reading bits of our poems out, they were mega-crap.

"That guy's going to do a real wobbly when he sees these," said Andy.

"Bet he doesn't come in smiling tomorrow," added Gaz. But he did.

"Thanks for all the poetry," said C.K.

"Enjoy it, did you?" called out Andy.

"I certainly did," replied C.K. "Won't say it's the best poetry I've ever read — but it shows great promise. It's lively, funny and original. Let me show you what I mean. Here's one from Greg Foord."

I started to do a beamer, both Gaz and Andy were cracking up already. Then Andy started squeezing my knee. "Don't get embarrassed, Jugger," he said laughing as C.K. goes – "Now Greg's poem is called *The Headmaster* and here it is.

Most of his day is over, his little light is out.
What used to be his sex appeal is now his water spout.
It used to be embarrassing to make the thing behave.
For nearly every morning it stood up and watched him shave.
But now he's on the downward slope and can't see past his middle.
And if he did, he'd have a shock – now he can hardly raise a wiggle.

The class clapped and whistled – especially the line about it standing up and watching him shave. And none laughed louder or clapped longer than C.K. He read several other poems aloud and seemed to be really enjoying each one.

"Tell you what," he said. "I'd like to make an anthology of your poems, they're so good." He brought out this really swish folder and some paper that looked expensive. Too good to write on, in fact. "So I'd be very grateful if you'd copy out your poems on this paper, then I can keep them."

"He's off his rocker," said Andy, but he and Gaz were scribbling away.

"Had no idea this poetry-writing was such a cinch," said Andy.

I took my poem home. Wanted to improve it. Spent half the night on it.

Did a lot of work for English, perhaps because C.K. never covered your work in red ink, unlike most teachers. Instead, he'd ask you what you wanted him to do with your work. I said he could make a paper aeroplane out of it if he wanted. He laughed. He laughed a lot. Only teacher who seemed to enjoy himself. You never heard him shout, he never gave detentions. Used to say, "Extra time spent with me is a pleasure not a punishment." Laughed as he said it, of course.

Liked to tell stories too. Had a story for every occasion. Don't know if I believed them all but he was good company and a good teacher. Then one Saturday Andy and I saw him down at Wycombe. Most teachers jump into a shop and hide if they spot a pupil. Not C.K. Even though he had his arm round a girl. Quite a tasty one too. Instead, he introduced us to her. Like we were mates. She was called Pippa, thought she'd have a funny name like that.

"Fancy a coffee?" said C.K.

Over coffee he told us that he and Pippa had met at the university and were now going steady.

"Bet he's given her one," whispered Andy.

"Bound to have," I whispered back.

C.K. was the only teacher I could ever imagine going on the job.

"Do you two live together?" I asked.

There was a silence.

"Or perhaps I shouldn't ask," I said.

"Oh no, no," said Pippa. "It's just this is a subject we've often discussed."

"Oh," I felt rather awkward.

"But at the moment," interrupted C.K., "it's impossible. Pippa's a solicitor in London and I'm obviously teaching here."

"Get a job in London," said Andy.

"Thank you, Andy," said Pippa, "that's exactly what I say."

"Don't want to teach in London," mumbled C.K.

"Couldn't be any bigger dumps than our school," said Andy.

"You'd be surprised," murmured C.K.

"So where do you live?" I asked.

"Just off Rose Avenue, Daglish Lane. I live with a very old couple . . ."

"Who wash his clothes, cook his meals," interrupted Pippa.

"And let me win at cards. Won 20p last night."

"So you only see Pippa at weekends," said Andy. "I don't

think I could bear that." He was flirting like mad now. He flirts with anyone, even my mum. Pippa played up to him.

"Thank you, Andy, I'm glad someone appreciates me."

"C.K., why don't you get yourself a proper job?" continued Andy.

"It is a proper job," said C.K. "Why, teaching can be the most exciting job in the world."

Was he joking? You never knew.

"That's crap," said Andy, then looking at Pippa, he goes, "Sorry."

"That's all right," said Pippa. "Chris, I mean C.K., does talk a lot of crap."

"But not in this case," said C.K. "Teachers are very lucky people. They can go on enjoying the teenage years over and over. And make no mistake, the teenage years are the best."

"As you can see," said Pippa, "your teacher is just a big kid." She was smiling as she said it; at least, I think she was.

A week later C.K. passed Smokers' Wall at break-time.

"Fags out. Teacher," shouted a look-out.

"No, it's all right," said Andy. "It's not a teacher – it's C.K. Just carry on, it'll be okay."

The other smokers were a bit apprehensive. A teacher, even a tame teacher, was still the enemy, could still turn nasty.

As C.K. drew nearer, Andy called out, "All right, C.K."

"All right, mate," goes C.K.

"Don't mind us fagging away," said Andy.

"No," said C.K. "My eyes are closed. Anyway, they're doing just the same in the staffroom. Only," he paused, "the company's better here." Andy flashed his fags. "Want a ciggie?" he said to C.K.

"Well, er . . ."

"Go on, have a social fag."

"All right, then," said C.K. "Just one. Don't tell anyone, though, get me shot."

Of course, we never told any teachers – but the story went

round the school, mighty exaggerated too. Soon the rumour was that C.K. had been seen with the lads, smoking.

Quite often C.K. joined us at break-time, chatted after school. Yet, no one took advantage in his lessons. We liked him, wanted to keep in with him. Were proud of him, in fact. Especially of his trendy clothes. Not sure who wrote C.K. RULES, OK on the Smokers' Wall. Could have been any of us.

Then, one November day, when C.K. had been at school about two months, I achieved the impossible. I got C.K. mad.

At the beginning of English, C.K. looked a bit hung-over.

"Busy night," said Andy.

"Very," said C.K. "She wouldn't leave me alone – this woman in my dream, I mean."

"Bet you woke up wet," said Andy.

"Soaking," replied C.K.

You could laugh around with C.K. Good way of starting the lesson, really woke you up. But C.K.'s laughing seemed forced. He was obviously really knackered. Then, he did the register, slower than usual, and when he came to Gaz he looked around, "Anyone seen old Gaz?" he said.

"He's at the dentist," I said. I really thought he was.

"Poor devil. Okay, thanks, Jugger."

Ten minutes later, who walks in – but Gaz.

"More fillings," calls out C.K.

Gaz looks blank. "What?"

"Dentist, just been to the dentist, haven't you?"

"No, I went to Matron at break-time."

C.K. stared at me, then Gaz. A new note crept into his voice. "Decided not to skive off after all, did you, Gaz?"

"I've been at Matron's," said Gaz, shocked at C.K.'s tone.

C.K. sat behind – rather than on – his desk. Something I'd never seen him do before. Then his voice shook as he went, "There's one thing, just one thing I hate and that's being lied to." He was staring right at me.

"What are you looking at me for?" I said.

"Because I've caught you and Gaz out. You want to get your stories right next time." Then he started ranting on, like a real teacher. "It's typical, isn't it. You're quite happy for me to be good to you. But, despite all I do I'm still – the enemy, aren't I?"

He sounded hysterical. Reminded me of Bogie. But no one laughed at C.K. getting mad. I couldn't even answer him – too confused, too angry, too upset. At the end of the lesson I was going to go up to him but he gave me such a foul look I turned away.

Then Gaz comes up. "Cheers for covering for me, mate, but if I was going to do a bunk it wouldn't be from a C.K. lesson."

"Look, I really thought you were at the dentist. Didn't you mention going to the dentist?"

"I said about the receptionist at my dentist and that if I wasn't going out with Debs, reckon I could be in there."

"That must be it, then." I'd made a mistake, but C.K. had been well out of order.

"You really got up C.K.'s bum," said Andy that night. "He was in a funny mood all day."

"More fool him. C.K.'s totally in the wrong."

"Oh yeah, yeah," said Andy. "Still, C.K. is normally a good bloke and I suppose it did look a bit suspicious, you saying Gaz was at the dentist, then him walking in with a totally different story."

We were sitting on the fence by Hazlemere Crossroads. Andy jumped down. "Sore bum," he yells. Then he says, "Why don't we go round C.K.'s house and talk to him about it."

"Don't know where he lives."

"Yeah, we do. Daglish Avenue, end house. Lives with two old fossils."

51

"We can't just go round."

"Why not. Could be a laugh. Besides I've never been round a teacher's house."

"He might not let us in."

"Bet he does. He probably feels bad about what happened. Wants to make up."

"Well . . ."

"Come on, mate. We're not doing anything else."

Found C.K.'s house easily. A male fogey drew away some curtains, unlocked the bolts and tottered before us. Didn't quite go with C.K.'s image, living here.

"Is Chris in?" I asked.

"Yes," said fogey.

"Can we see him?"

He stared at us. Don't think he was very impressed. "He's boiling the kettle," he said. Then he added, "Who shall I say is calling?"

"Two friends," I said.

He stared at us again. Then closed the door, drew the curtain, too.

A few seconds later the curtain was drawn back again, door opened and C.K. stood there, shirt hanging out, looking as if he'd just woken up. He stared at us in amazement.

"Can we have a word?" asked Andy.

"Sure, come through."

We followed him into a very dingy room, all drab colours and hard chairs. He motioned us to sit down. Before we could say anything the female species of the fossil family staggered through — "Excuse me," she said, giving us a long, hard look.

"Where's she going?" asked Andy.

"You have to go through my room to get to the loo, it's on past the kitchen."

"Must be a bit of a nuisance," I said.

"It is," replied C.K.

A look of sympathy passed between us. The atmosphere relaxed.

"We came round," I said, "because you seemed worked up this morning." I sounded as if I was delivering a speech. I hate this sort of conversation. I tried to soften my tone as I added, "And I didn't lie to you. I really thought Gaz was at the dentist."

"I know, I know," said C.K. "And I owe you both – especially Jugger – an apology." But he still didn't sound himself: not narked any more, but distant, far away.

"Jugger's been all in a sweat today," said Andy. "All worked up because you didn't believe him."

I blushed. C.K. looked touched – and embarrassed.

"I feel really bad," he said. "Today, I committed the cardinal sin of teaching. I took my anger out on you. When really, I was angry about something quite different."

"What?" asked Andy.

Before C.K. could answer, Mrs Fogey was back with us, her bowels now empty but her eyes as full of curiosity as ever.

"Help your guests," she emphasized that last word, "to tea or coffee if you wish, Christopher."

"Thanks, Mrs Cooper."

As the door closed C.K. said, "Does anyone want a coffee or tea?"

"What about something stronger?" said Andy. He said it as a dare. Was always asking questions like that. He asked my mum if she wanted to play strip poker once. However, to our great amazement, C.K. took Andy seriously.

"Well, I'll tell you, I had a little nip of whisky earlier."

"And you know what they say about people who drink alone," bantered Andy.

"Exactly, exactly," said C.K. He was becoming all keyed up again. "So if I get the whisky, perhaps you can get some coke out of the fridge. Just fancy a whisky and coke."

He tore upstairs like a little kid who's been asked out to a party. Andy burst into the fridge. "See these pies, do you think C.K. would mind if I heated one up?"

"Yes, I do," I replied. "Can't go eating him out of house and home. Just bring the coke like you were told."

"We're not at school now, you know," said Andy, reluctantly closing the fridge. "Tell you, Jugger, I'm going to enjoy myself tonight."

By now C.K. had sprinted downstairs, carrying a large bottle of whisky. "Glasses, glasses," he said, all frantic and excited as he dived into an ancient brown cupboard. Then he poured generous measures of whisky into three wine glasses – and picked up the coke bottle.

"Say when," he said.

"Actually, C.K. I prefer it neat," said Andy.

That was a lie. A posy lie.

But C.K. goes, "What a man. Okay. I'll top you up with whisky, then."

"A teacher pouring me out a drink," said Andy. "Now there's a strange event."

"No, Andy, it's not an event," corrected C.K. "Out of school I'm just like you."

How old are you?" said Andy.

"Guess," said C.K.

"Forty," said Andy.

"Hey, hey."

"Fifty," I shouted.

"No. I'm six years older than you – that's all."

"Twenty-two," said Andy. "I'd never have thought that."

"Well, cheers, Andy."

"No, no," said Andy. "Actually you do look young. Could be a sixth former in fact."

We settled ourselves down in our hard chairs. "Mind if we smoke?" asked Andy.

"I don't but my landlady does. Says it gets in the curtains. Still, as this is rather a special occasion."

54

Andy looked at me. "I'm down to my last one. But you've got a new packet haven't you, Jugger? Settle with you tomorrow."

I knew Andy wouldn't. But I'm not mean. So I flashed my fags. C.K. took one too. Felt quite proud of that.

"Been trying to give up," said C.K. "Certainly cut down. But there are special moments where a ciggie is in order."

"Do you smoke after sex?" said Andy suddenly.

"Never looked," replied C.K.

Took Andy a few seconds to get the joke, then he goes, "Like it. Like It."

C.K. always had an answer.

C.K. knew a lot of jokes too. Real corny ones like: "What goes in dry and comes out wet? A tea-bag." But we laughed. We'd have laughed at anything that night. Especially Andy. He was already on his second whisky.

"This is good. Really good," said C.K. "Sitting here with two mates. Don't feel so bad any more."

"You never told us," I said, "why you were so angry."

"Been chucked," said C.K. quickly. "Pippa rang me last night. Gave me the royal order of the boot." He smiled as he said it. But he wasn't really smiling.

"That's bad," said Andy. He let out a low whistle. "Come on C.K., drink up, you're falling behind." And Andy poured himself another drink. His third.

"Why did she chuck you?" I said quietly.

C.K. didn't answer at first, instead he seemed to go into a trance, then said, "She chucked me because . . . because she was tired of waiting for me to grow up. She wants to settle down, have a nice little house, 2.4 children, all the trappings – and I don't feel ready."

"You know what you want to do," said Andy breaking into C.K.'s thoughtful mood. "You want to get pissed and you won't get pissed on one glass." He topped C.K. up.

"Careful, careful, you're spilling it," I said.

Andy started giggling. "I'll top myself up now."

I tried to get back to C.K.'s problem. "I can see why you were well upset – Pippa chucking you and all. But, perhaps she didn't mean it."

"She meant it," said C.K.

"Jugger knows all about chucking," slurred Andy. "He chucks girls after one date. Tell me, C.K., have any of the staff ever dropped 'em for you," and Andy started laughing really loudly. "What about old Ma Davies, has she ever dropped 'em?"

"No staff have offered," said C.K., mock sadly. "Female teachers are interested in only three things: babies, cooking and slimming."

"Oh, shit," said Andy, standing up suddenly. "C.K., your bog's through the kitchen, isn't it?"

"Yes, straight through. Do you feel bad?"

Andy didn't answer, didn't have to. He just spewed up on the carpet. Then he charged into the loo – for more of the same, no doubt.

"God, he's almost finished the bottle," I said.

But C.K. was looking at something else – a generous helping of puke – glistening and glowing, as it lay in the lamp light.

Made me want to retch just looking at it.

"Oh no," moaned C.K. "They'll go mad when they see this."

I nodded.

"I'd better clear it up."

I nodded again.

"Er, how do you think I should do that?"

"Could always get Andy to do it. His fault."

"No, no, I'll do it. I was just wondering how?"

"You could do what a mate of mine did, hoover it up."

"Hoover it," said C.K. "Mm, yes, yes, why not. Now where is the hoover. Oh yes, under the stairs." He opened his door. Could hear the TV blaring away in the fogeys' room. This camouflaged the noise of C.K. easing the hoover out of the cupboard and back into his room.

"Get the telly on, Jugger," said C.K. I put it on the same

channel as the fogeys'. It was one of those quiz shows where the audience clap and cheer if the contestant gets his name right. Then C.K. switched on the hoover. The hoover didn't seem to appreciate the lumps of puke it had to pick up. And the slushy noise the vomit made as it was sucked up, turned my stomach.

A horrible manky mess remained. And, as for the smell!

"I'll have to try to soak it up," said C.K., running into the kitchen to get a cloth. He came back. "I'll buy them a new cloth tomorrow." Certainly, that cloth couldn't be used again.

"I'd better go and see what Andy's doing," I said. Although I could guess.

The toilet door was locked.

"All right, Andy?"

"Yeah, go away. I'll be out in a minute."

"Have you . . .?"

"Yeah. Tell C.K. he needs some more bog roll."

"Okay." I went back into the lounge. C.K. was scrubbing the carpet, whilst the audience on the quiz show were shouting and whistling and screaming. And they complain about kids!

But worst of all, was the smell. "It reeks in here," I said.

C.K. stood up. "Jugger, I can't seem to get rid of the stain. Do you want to have a go?"

"No thanks."

"Tell you what, then," said C.K., "go into my bedroom, it's first on your right, and bring down all the deodorants you can find."

Two minutes later, I came down, laden with C.K.'s smellies. We both started spraying them around the room, kept on until we began coughing. "Have we hidden the sick smell?" asked C.K.

"I'd say, replaced it, with an even worse smell."

C.K. looked worried. You'd have thought the fogeys were his parents and he was our age.

"And there's still the stain," he said sadly. "Can't seem to get that up."

"Tell you what," I said. "If we move that table over the stain they probably won't notice. While we heaved the table, Andy reappeared. Tiny globules of sick hung on his lip. He looked terrible.

"Wipe your mouth, Andy," I said briskly.

He fell into a chair, shoved his sleeve over his mouth and muttered, "I want to go home."

"How far's he got to go?" asked C.K.

"Holmer Green, about two miles," I said.

"I'll get a taxi," said C.K.

"No, no, we'll be okay. I'll get him home."

"No, let me get you a taxi," argued C.K. "I've got a directory here."

But Andy settled it by staggering to his feet and declaring, "I'm going home now."

"Do you still feel bad, Andy?" asked C.K.

He nodded.

"I think he might throw up again," I said. "Probably better if we go now."

"Well, if you're sure."

"I'll look after him," I said. We propelled Andy towards the door.

"Sorry about – everything," I said, patting C.K. on the back.

"Smell's not too bad, now, is it?" asked C.K. anxiously.

I felt really sorry for him. "No, no, anyway, they're old, so they probably won't have a very good sense of smell."

Any further discussion was cut short by Andy throwing up on the next-door neighbour's wall.

"I'll get him home – quick," I said. "And cheers for a good evening – before . . ."

"Yes, it was a good evening, wasn't it?" said C.K. He smiled. Only ever saw him smile once more.

Walking Andy home was extremely tiring and extremely

boring. Unfortunately, he hung on to me. I say unfortunately, because the smell Andy gave off was not a pretty one and he was talking rubbish. All about some slag he fancied. "You know, Jugger, she's the only girl I really care for. In fact, I love her."

"Yeah, yeah."

It was really nippy and I was feeling well knackered. "Come on, speed up."

"No, honestly, mate, I love that little girl. Well, she's not that little. But I love her – and I'm going to tell her now."

"What a load of bollocks," I snapped.

He wrenched himself free from me. "And you can sod off," he shouted. Before I realized it, he'd marched away, all indignant.

"Where are you going?" I called.

"I'm going to see her now."

"But she lives down Penn."

"Great," said Andy. "But you needn't come with me, in fact I'd prefer it if you didn't."

He stormed down Penn Road. I should have followed him. Meant to. But Andy was really getting up my nose. And the last thing I wanted was to follow Andy all the way to Penn. No, he'd be all right. He always was – and I was cold, tired and pissed off. So I left him and went home.

Next morning, I was woken up by my mum and a policeman. Mum sat on the bed. The policeman stood over me. He had a notebook out.

"This is a policeman," said my mum rather unnecessarily. "He wants to ask you some questions." She sounded frightened.

"I would like you to tell me what you did last night?" He spoke slowly. As if he was talking to a mental.

"I went out about eight o'clock with, um, Andy Horne, and I got back about half past eleven." I was speaking like a mental. Terrified.

"Where had you been?"

"To see a – friend."

"Name and address, please."

"Well, not exactly a friend – we went to see a teacher."

"Name, address."

"Mr Kenting. Lives down Daglish Lane, just off Rose Avenue."

"And tell me, Greg, how much alcohol was consumed at Mr Kenting's."

"What?" Just where was this leading.

"I repeat, Greg, how much alcohol was drunk at Mr Kenting's?"

"A bit," I croaked.

"How much is a bit?"

"About half a glass of whisky. Really small measures . . . but why – why are you asking all this?"

His tone grew harsh. "Because your friend, Andrew Horne, was found lying in a garden – unconscious and naked – at one o'clock this morning."

I started breathing really quickly. Like someone who's been holding his breath for too long.

"And if the owner of the garden hadn't noticed Andrew Horne, he'd probably have died of exposure by now."

"Where is. . . ?"

"Wycombe hospital. I spoke to him about half an hour ago. He's still in a very weak state and remembers very little of last night. But I know he'd been drinking heavily, very heavily. And so I want to know exactly what pubs you visited. I can check – but I'd rather you told me." My mum's eyes bored into me. The policeman towered over me. I was being tried, in my own bedroom.

"We didn't visit any pubs," I said.

"Are you sure?"

I nodded. Later, I wished I'd lied – but I was too confused to think properly.

"So, Andrew Horne became excessively drunk as a result of what he'd consumed at your teacher's house?"

60

My mum started making "tut, tutting" noises.

"How much did your teacher offer Andrew Horne to drink?"

"Only one glass. But Andy helped himself – when Mr Kenting wasn't looking."

P.C. Plod wasn't buying this. Instead, he lowered his voice, "Greg, are you in the habit of going round to teachers' houses?"

"No."

"Yet, this teacher invites you two around to his house, and offers you unlimited drink . . . tell me, has this teacher been showing you any special attention?"

I knew which way his mind was working. Dirty-minded sod. I began to get angry. "Actually, he invited me around because he'd just split up with his girlfriend."

"And why does that concern you?" The policeman's voice was all soft and creepy. He was determined to find something sinister in all this.

"Why shouldn't he discuss his problems with me. He's a young teacher and he hasn't got many mates . . ."

"Really," said the policeman. He was scribbling down everything I said.

After he left, a second interrogation from my mum. "Why did you go round his house? Does he live alone? Why did he give you all that drink?"

I couldn't explain it to her. And when I said, "Poor C.K.," she went, "Poor Andy, you mean, he's the one in hospital, thanks to your teacher's negligence."

"Mum, how many more times. Andy behaved like a kid, ruined our evening . . . it was his fault."

"Your teacher was in charge of you. He should have stopped Andy." Unfortunately, at that moment my mum picked up my trousers – which I'd left on the floor last night – and out rolled my packet of ciggies.

"You've been smoking, too," said Mum. She pretended not to know I smoked. "I suppose the teacher gave you these."

61

It saved time to agree. "Yes, Mum, he did."

"He ought to be struck off, this teacher of yours, he's a disgrace, an absolute disgrace."

I didn't see C.K. in school that day. He'd been sighted but apparently he'd spent most of the day in the Head's office. I could guess what was going on there. However, I saw Andy after school – lying in a hospital bed, grinning all over his face, yelling, "The nurses in here are, well horny."

I was relieved that Andy was okay and I do like him, most of the time. But I also felt angry that he was so happy while I and C.K. had gone through hell.

"You've caused a right mess, you have."

Andy grinned.

"So what happened to you last night?"

"It's all a blank," he said dramatically.

"Crap."

"Jugger." He sounded hurt. He was obviously expecting me to be laden with grapes and sympathy. "You really piss me off," I said. "I suppose you realize all the hassle you've caused."

"Keep your voice down, mate. Help yourself to a chocolate," he added, placing a huge box in front of me.

"It's all right for you, isn't it, with all this attention and sympathy and chocolates . . . bloody chocolates." I punched the box hard. The chocolates all flew on to the floor while Andy sat up, mouth open, that stupid hurt look on his face again. "Suppose you realize," I continued, "I've had the pigs round, my mum's gone up the wall and when I go home I've got my dad to face. I probably won't be allowed out for a month. And as for C.K., you've really fouled him up." I was screaming at him and my head was pounding as if in accompaniment.

"Now what's all this?" said a nurse whose voice was as starched as her uniform.

I didn't answer her. Couldn't. But as I left I heard Andy shout, "Bet you wish you'd seen me home, don't you, Jugger."

I wished a lot of things, but mainly I wished I could look C.K. in the face. He seemed afraid to talk to me, deliberately leaving his classroom straight after lessons. Perhaps he'd been warned not to talk to me.

Then, a few days' later, he didn't leap away, so I purposely hung behind.

"How are you, Jugger?" he said, as if he hadn't seen me for a while.

"I'm okay," I said. "What about you?"

He sat on the desk, his favourite teaching position. "I feel better today," he said. "Much better."

"Is everything sorted out?" I asked.

"Yes, I think it is. I leave at the end of term."

"You got the sack?" I'd been dreading that.

"No, no, it's mutual."

"What will you do?"

"Pippa rang me last night, she's got a friend in advertising, she's got me an interview."

"Are you two back together?"

"Let's say we're talking . . . how's Andy?"

"Back at school tomorrow. I'm really sorry about that night."

"No, no it was my fault."

"No, we let you down. You treated us like mates . . ."

"Perhaps I had no right treating you as mates." He jumped up. "Will miss it, though. Love having my own classroom, being with you lot. It's all the rest of the crap I can't take – like not saying crap in front of a pupil."

He walked to the door.

"Bet we get a real gormo in your place," I said.

"Probably." He switched off the lights.

I suddenly thought. "Did those geriatrics you live with ever find out about the sick?"

C.K. smiled. "Oh yeah. We forgot one thing, to check the kitchen. It seems, on the way to the loo, Andy threw up in a bowl in the kitchen. A bowl which contained all their knickers."

"Oh no," I said, laughing.

"Yes, my landlady was most upset. I don't know if she actually found little globules of puke in her pants when she was trying them on."

By now we were both laughing loudly and getting a funny look from the caretaker, waiting outside.

"Can you imagine her," I said "putting on her pants and finding . . ." We both cracked up again.

The caretaker was jangling his keys loudly. C.K. opened the door. But before he left I extended my hand to him. We shook hands.

"Why are we shaking hands?" asked C.K.

"Don't know," I said. "Just wanted to say thank you."

"For what?" said C.K.

"For being a good bloke," I replied.

C.K. didn't answer, almost ran to his car. But I'd swear he was crying.

P.S.

Yonks later I got a card from C.K. saying he was at an advertising agency and really coining it in. When I told Andy he said, "There you are. We did him a favour getting him sacked!"

Wish I could agree.

And now, "for something completely different", I've just discovered Monty Python – it's nearly as funny as the weather forecast. Firstly, when is a story not a story? When it's a log!!

I'll explain that. You know how when people go up the Amazon or down past Watford they keep a day-to-day log of their trip – well this is an actual authentic log I kept when I thought I was travelling up . . . No, that's crude!

Anyhow, reading this log earlier tonight, I thought what a load of . . . and tried to rewrite it. Couldn't, so I thought, what the hell, you may as well see it all, even the cringy bits – on one condition: don't laugh at me too much!!

Log / Day One / Friday

Tonight, a miracle happened. To be precise, the miracle occurred at 10.43 p.m. That was when Gaz took Lizzie upstairs. Still can't believe it. You see, for the past three hundred and fifty-eight days, Gaz has been going out with Debbie Arnold. They've been the 5th year's most talked about clique.

But tonight – at Rubi's party – Gaz and this Lizzie "something" (girl from the High School) were upstairs, pumping away. No good Gaz denying it. There's evidence. For Andy actually snapped them together, a real action shot apparently. Very cruel of Andy, of course, but the photo should be epic.

And a real crack! Not that Gaz was laughing. Not at all. It's the first time Debbie and he have been separated (Debbie's grandad's getting re-married so she's away until Sunday) and when Debbie returns and hears about Gaz's close encounter – and I know at least a hundred people who can't wait to tell her – their separation could be permanent.

Leaving Debbie free to fall into whose arms? Go on, guess.

Ever since Debbie first went out with Gaz I've fancied her, madly, insanely. I've tried to forget her. Been out with scores of other girls. But they made it worse. It's like when you watch support groups at a concert – all they do is make you more and more desperate for the main act.

And yes, I've been growing desperate. You see, I had this wild idea that Debbie and Gaz would go on going out together . . . dates unending, until they got engaged and all the rest. That's why tonight's coupling is an earth-shattering miracle.

However, I won't make a move at Debbie until the

chucking takes place. Feel mean even thinking about it, especially as Gaz is a mate. But still, if Debbie doesn't go out with me it will be someone else (someone far less deserving) and Gaz will soon get fixed up again (loads of girls fancy him), and besides, going out with the same girl for a whole year is indecent. Stunts your sexual growth.

No, a change will do everyone some good. Especially me. Can't write any more, panting too much.

Log / Day Two / Saturday

Gaz has just been round, giving me a right earful. Never seen him so mad. Not at me – but at Andy. Reckons Andy and some other mates set him up last night. Gaz said he never wanted to go to Rubi's party but Andy begged him. Said if he didn't go he was letting the lads down, all that stuff.

So Gaz goes – for half an hour. Only his drinks are spiked. Convinced of that. Soon Gaz is out of his skull. He remembers going outside and dancing with some trees. Then this bird he's never seen before (none of us have – must be a friend of Rubi's), Lizzie something, slinks over, all friendly like and says, "I dance better than the trees."

They amble around treading on each other's toes, Gaz says, "Actually, I think the trees dance better than you," and she laughs and drags him into the kitchen.

While she spills Gaz another drink, he pukes up all over the floor. So then he and Lizzie crouch in the corner, sniggering at all the people sliding on the sick as they slip (!!) into the kitchen. The rest, Gaz says, is a blur. He remembers passing out. When I said, "How can you remember passing out?" Gaz said he recalls feeling gutted and woozy – and then he recalls lying on a floor and a bright light punching his throbbing head; that's the flash from Andy's camera.

If Gaz's story is true I can see why he is so wound up. Apparently, Debbie's arriving back on Sunday afternoon and Gaz aims to get to her before any of her friends do. Tricky.

"If I can tell her the truth before her so-called friends, all will be well," were Gaz's exact words to me.

I'm nodding saying, "I hope it all works out, Gaz," while secretly, hoping it won't. Talk about snidey.

More fireworks when I repeated Gaz's story to Andy.

"He was on the job," said Andy. "Not that I blame him – I mean what guy's going to turn it down when it's on offer."

"A guy who's got a steady girlfriend."

Andy shook his head. "As for all that crap about passing out." He paused, "I'll just say for someone who'd passed out, Gaz was moving around a lot."

Anyway, proof positive on Tuesday. That was when Andy's photo would be developed.

Not sure if I believe Gaz or Andy. Or perhaps they're both telling porky pies. Still, doesn't matter what I think. It's what Debbie thinks, that counts – and she's back tomorrow.

Log / Day Three / Sunday

Morning was dead, what Sunday morning isn't, and the afternoon tense. For Gaz had said he'd ring me as soon as he'd seen Debbie about Friday's fiasco (Gaz's words). All afternoon I was waiting by the phone, hoping for the worst. Then, just after four o'clock Gaz rings me. Hardly recognized his voice, it was so low and hoarse. Perhaps he'd been shouting. For the news was bad.

"Refuses to see me. I've been round, rung, but no go."

"Someone's got to her."

"Guess what, one of her dear 6th form friends flagged the car down in Wycombe."

"That's wicked." (Incidentally, Debbie is a 6th former too; yes, she's one year older than Gaz and me.)

"What will you do now?"

"Thought of camping outside her house. Might even get a banner, 'I am the Truth'."

That sounded crazy but good. Too good. "No, I wouldn't do that."

"Why?"

"She's obviously mad, you picketing her house would just get her madder. No, give her time to cool down."

"But those bitches might be telling her more lies about me. I could picket Jo Martin's house."

"Why her house?"

"Because that's where Deb's gone."

"What, for a sob and a gossip?"

"Probably. But also to cancel our party."

"Oh yeah."

Next Friday is Gaz and Debbie's anniversary – a year to the day they first stepped out together. Jo Martin is giving a special party to celebrate this mind-blowing event. Or rather she was.

"So I'll go round," began Gaz.

"No, leave it all to me, Gaz. I'll put the record straight for you."

"Really."

"No sweat. I'm off to Jo Martin's now."

"And will you ring me as soon as you get back?"

"The very second."

I togged myself up in a clean white shirt and new jeans (look better in casual clothes) and didn't give myself time to reflect on how falsely I was behaving. I set off for Jo's house. Know it well. She gives about a party a fortnight. Think she was surprised to see me. And yet, there was just a whisper of a smile as she said, "Hello, Greg."

"Hello, Jo. Is Debbie here?"

"Yes."

"Could I see her?"

Jo stepped outside, putting the door on the catch, then hissed, "Don't think she's in a fit state to see anyone. Nearly gone through one box of tissues already . . . and she's far from finished." Jo said it almost proudly.

"How long's she been crying?"

"She's not crying, she's got a nose bleed. Said shock brought it on. The shock of Mandy Lake and Mandy's spotty boyfriend waving her family car down, inviting Debbie for a drink and telling her ALL."

Tried to imagine Debbie upset. Impossible. Didn't connect with my image of a cool blonde with a determined chin and a body that belonged in a centre fold. I could imagine Debbie sipping cocktails, parachuting from planes, travelling the world, becoming a film star, but speeding through Jo's tissues nose bleeding away – never.

"Gaz asked me to come round to explain about . . ."

"Yes."

"But you don't think this would be a good time?"

"No, but I'll tell her you called. Perhaps she'll see you later."

"Yes."

"I just hope it all works out," Jo sighed.

"Yes."

"I'm so worried about it all."

"Yes."

"I mean, I've already made arrangements."

"Arrangements?" It was a relief to say something other than "Yes".

"For Friday. I've hired a group. My cousin's group. They've re-arranged their schedule to come down specially. So I don't want to cancel the party."

"No. Well, perhaps they'll have made up by Friday – or found new partners."

Jo gave me a funny look. Shouldn't have made that last comment.

"Anyway, if Debbie does want to speak, let me know."

Jo nodded. But she didn't say anything else. She just stood on the step, watching me leave. Made me feel all self-conscious. I put my hands in my pockets and started whistling. Jo kept on watching me. Had she guessed I fancied Debby. Must be more careful.

Later that night Gaz rang me. "Any news?"

"No, that's why I didn't call you. She refused to see me but I haven't given up."

"Well, if that's the way she wants to play it, she can. Anyhow, I've finished with her."

"Don't be too hasty," I said, half-heartedly.

"No, I'm sick of her, of the whole mess. We're through."

Never had Monday looked so good.

Log / Day Four / Monday

Writing this really fast – don't want to miss anything, not a millicentimetre, of what happened during my best Monday ever.

Day began at five to four in the afternoon. For school was the usual numbing nothing but at five to four I was looking for my Maths book (Andy'd borrowed it but couldn't remember where he'd put it) so I quickly opened my locker door – always open my locker quickly because of the whiff of stale socks and sandwiches – and was about to close it again when . . . I forgot my Maths book, forgot everything. For there was a piece of notepaper – the sort I normally cringe at – all four-year-old girls and revoltingly cute kittens – but not then. Not ever, now. As on the notepaper was a message. The first from my beloved. RING H.W. 712840 TONIGHT. DEBBIE.

Then an agonizing decision. What time does "Tonight" mean? When does "Tonight" begin – six o'clock, seven o'clock? Had to get it right. Finally decided, tonight meant straight after school. So, two seconds into my house I was phoning.

"Remember, it's the expensive time," said my mum.

I ignored her and rang H.W. 712840.

"Hello," a strange voice answered.

"Hello, who is that?"

Voice said something else. Sounded foreign or mental.

"Hello, Hello."

No answer.

"Hello."

"Hello," Debbie's voice at last.

"Oh, hello, it's Greg, thought I'd got a wrong number."

"No, it was me. I was eating a biscuit."

"Ah."

"A chocolate biscuit."

"Good."

"Pardon."

"I said, 'Good'."

"Why?"

"Er, good you were eating a chocolate biscuit. I like chocolate biscuits."

"Good. Can you pop round tonight?"

"Yes, sure."

"Seven o'clock?"

"Perfect."

"See you then."

"Sure and thanks for ringing."

I'm not normally a dick. Quite the opposite. A great yarner, in fact. But while I was talking to her on the phone my brain gave out. Must make sure that doesn't happen tonight.

So I rehearsed what I was going to say to Debbie. Gotta be cool, smooth, macho. I also decided I would put Gaz's case to Debbie. Just as I'd promised him. That was only fair. Estimated that would take about ten minutes, leaving the rest of the evening for . . .

Of course, I arrived far too early. So I did a couple of turns round the block. Then a couple more. It was still only twenty five past six. So I sat on a bench by the library and practised my lines.

As my watch struck seven my hand struck Debbie's bell. Her little brother answered – ten years old, going on forty. "Oh, do come in. I believe Deborah is in the lounge. Follow me. Heel."

"What?" Then I realized he was talking to the dog.

He opened the lounge. "Deborah, your guest has arrived."

Debbie smiles and motions me to a chair. She's perched on the settee: knees clasped to her ample bosom. She's got a yellow top on and a grey skirt. A tight grey skirt. I stare and drool. A very tight grey skirt.

"Hello, Greg." Her voice is husky and matches the very tight grey skirt.

"Evening, Debbie." I keep my voice casual.

"Greg."

There she goes saying my name again.

"Will you take a message to Gaz for me?"

I nod. Don't trust myself to speak.

"Tell him we're finished. He's not to ring me, try to see me at school – not anything. Got that."

I nod again.

"Thank you, Greg. I'm sorry you've been dragged into this, but if you tell him what I've said that should be it."

She stopped talking and looked at the clock over my head. My audience with her was at an end. But I wasn't going that soon. I was determined to stretch this dream out. "Actually, I've got a message for you from Gaz."

Her eyes were on me again.

"His message to you is very similar to the one you gave me for him. Identical in fact."

72

Her eyes urged me on. "He said he was sick of you, and you and he were through."

Her eyes flashed with anger. I said quickly, "But he feels you misunderstood Friday's fiasco."

"I didn't misunderstand anything."

"No, he just thought you over-reacted to what you heard – perhaps because you were so upset . . ."

"Upset! Is that what he thinks?" She smiled. "Oh, the fool, the utter fool. Do you know what I did when I heard about Gaz and that sleese-bag? I laughed, I laughed for an hour."

"Really." I knew this was a lie.

"I'd been dying to break up with him for ages. Now I had the perfect excuse."

This time I couldn't even nod.

"You don't believe me?" her voice rose.

"Well, it is a little hard to understand. I mean, you and he were so close."

Her voice became confiding. "I'm going to tell you the truth about Gaz and me. I shouldn't but I'm going to. If you want to know."

I nodded frantically.

"All right, then. First of all his feet smell. Reek. And when he takes his shoes off – it's like a major gas attack – I've tried swamping his shoes in foot odour powder. But it's hopeless, hopeless. Next there's Gaz's nose. Have you ever heard him blow his nose? Deafening. And he does it over and over. Usually just before he kisses me. As for our loo, Gaz lives in there. Mum reckons he's got permanent diarrhoea. He's got something wrong down there. And then he farts. Sneaky, quiet, deadly ones. He tries to blame it on our dog, Holly, so poor Holly is put outside. But Holly never farts except when she's had chicken . . . I wish I could remember everything," Debbie said. But she went on for ages. Her last story I do recall. "Last summer I was in Paris, with my father, when this gentleman, quite elderly but very distinguished looking, came over and kissed my hand. They do that in France. And he said I was a most beautiful young girl." Debbie glowed as she remembered the experience. "And he asked if he might give Father and me a little light refreshment and I said *Certainement*, and everyone laughed and he was so charming . . . Anyway, last November I was walking along the Octagon with Gaz when I saw him. The French gentleman. I waved. He waved. Then he kissed my hand again – so politely – and I introduced him to Gaz and do you know what Gaz said, "When are you going home?" So rude – so obvious." She shuddered. "So there's no way I could have gone on with Gaz. I mean, imagine the problems when I become a model."

"You're going to become a model?"

"Probably. Everyone says I should. We'll see. But you can see why I want to finish with Gaz. He's so immature. You'd think he was five years younger than me not one. And yet I didn't want to hurt him. Mind you, I'm saddened our relationship has to finish – how I hate that word finish – in such a rude, squalid way."

She pressed out her lower lip, sighed and released a tear. A great pearl of a tear. I felt like applauding.

That night I didn't sleep at all. People said Debbie Arnold was a poser, really false, affected, stuck up . . . she was all of these things and more. Yet she was also magnificent. Most girls are so drab, so basic, so usual, you can suss them out in five minutes. But Debbie – you'd never quite know where she was at. Never.

Yet when she looked at you, you stayed looked at, all night. Does that sound corny. I fear it does. But it's hard to write sensibly about someone who you . . . Oh, what the hell, I love her, I love her. At her house I'd wanted to declare my undying love for her, as well as tell her my feet don't smell, that I can spend hours without going to the loo and I only fart when I'm with Andy. But I didn't. Not yet. I'll lay a bet with myself though, before the week is out Debbie will be mine.

Log / Day Five / Tuesday

One day, the first words Debbie hears when she wakes will be mine saying, "I love you". I can imagine the scene, she lying beside me, hair flowing over the pillow, eyes half-closed, tits trembling, legs apart as she whispers, "Enter me" or knowing Debbie,"*Entré, entré*".

Before this happy event could transpire I had to ensure Gaz was off the scene. Despite all Debbie said I didn't think she was over Gaz yet. But as my mum says, "Time is a great healer". And there's always Andy's photo.

Andy was late for school because he waited for the chemist to open so he could bring his "snap trophy" first thing. He needn't have bothered. Big anti-climax. It was just a fuzzy, out of focus picture of Gaz lying on the floor and Lizzie "Something" draped across him. But they both looked fast asleep. Perhaps something had happened – perhaps it hadn't. The picture didn't prove anything, except that Andy was a lousy photographer.

By now, however, Gaz and Debbie were so far apart it didn't matter. Saw Debbie at school a couple of times. We smiled – but didn't talk. I didn't want to use up all the conversation I'd worked out at 4.00 a.m.

And then in the evening I had a pint with Gaz down "The Boot". His idea. Would rather have been visiting Debbie again but felt I owed him this chat. Besides, I wanted to make Gaz realize it was all over between him and Debbie. For his own good, really.

"Sorry I couldn't invite you round my house," said Gaz, "but things are a bit frantic at the moment."

"The old step-mum playing up?"

"As usual. Accuses me of picking on her two little darlings."

Last year, Gaz's dad had re-married, an Australian woman with two ghastly dingoes. Step-mum and Gaz were enemies.

"Heard from your mum?"

"Postcard from Liverpool. Said, having a great time – but not wish you were here. Anyhow, hear you went round Deb's last night."

Privately, I wondered who'd told him, but I just said, "No joy, I'm afraid. Tried to tell her what you'd said."

"But she wouldn't listen. I know. She gets an idea into her head and that's it."

"Mmm. She gave me a message for you, though."

"Yeah." Gaz pretended to be fiddling with an ash-tray. "Is the message repeatable?"

One part of me couldn't wait to tell him. The other dreaded witnessing the fallout.

"Deb told me you and she are finished." I spoke really slowly as if I was having to pull the words out of myself. "And she doesn't want you to ring her or see her at school – or anything."

Gaz was peering intently at the ash-tray, like it was an antique he was trying to price.

"Anything else?"

"No – except . . ."

"Yes."

Really hadn't intended telling him all the rest – the smelly feet, the farting, etc. – but once I started I couldn't stop. I both hated doing it, and also found it exciting.

As I spouted, Gaz muttered exclamations like "The Cow" but it was only when I recounted the story about the French guy, Gaz actually spilt a little dirt.

"Where does she get off saying all that crap about me?" He put his hand through his hair and spoke into his arm like it was a microphone. "Real story is this. One day we're down Wycombe when we meet this amazingly old guy – the kind who's so old he's got about eleven sticks and an oxygen tent following – and she waves at him. I didn't think anything of it, she's always waving at people, trying to pretend she knows the entire population of Wycombe. But this guy, after staring at her for a while, stumbles over to her and she starts pretending this ancient relic – with about two teeth – is the great love of her life. It was so pathetic and all to get me jealous. She's always trying to get me jealous. Yet she's the jealous one. I've given up going to the pub with her, for if I so much as breathe on anyone, bloke or bird, she goes into a sulk."

He lowered his hand. "Anyway, that's all behind me now. So will you tell her I certainly won't try to get in contact with her, *ever*. Will you tell her that?" I couldn't wait to tell her that.

Log / Day Six / Wednesday

First shock of the day: Jo Martin telling me the Friday party is still on.

"But how come? I mean, they haven't made up?" I said, suddenly panicky.

"No, of course not." Jo gave me another look. Not exactly a funny look, but certainly a look. Once again I wondered if she suspected how I felt about Debbie – but all she actually said was, "No, it's just everyone thinks Debbie is in floods of tears because of the bust up with Gaz and she wants to show them she's not. So, if they see her at the party having a good time, they'll realize, won't they?"

"Yes, they will," I said, wondering who "they" were.

"So it's just going to be a general "Open House", only if Debbie goes it would be better if Gaz didn't." Jo looked at me, expectantly.

"I'll see what I can do."

"But you'll still come."

"Oh yes."

Jo smiled. Quite a nice smile actually. I smiled back. Now I had a target, a goal. I was going to attend Friday's party with Debbie, and hopefully Gaz wouldn't be there at all.

Set out to score at half past seven. That's when I received shock No. 2. For as I walked past Debbie's dining room window, I noticed the curtains weren't drawn and the light was on. So of course I looked in – you can't help it, can you – and I saw . . .

I saw Debbie, her mum, dad and precocious brother, all sitting round the table. Only they weren't eating – the table was bare – just staring at each other. You'd have thought they were having a seance. Perhaps they were. It certainly seemed dead (!!) peculiar. Especially the way they kept peering downwards. I didn't like to interrupt. But I kept taking sneaky looks.

Then I went for yet another walk round the block. Felt like a policeman doing his beat. When I returned the curtains were drawn. Still felt uneasy about knocking and going in, until I saw their door open and Debbie's mum, dad and brother spring out. They all had tracksuits on – Debbie's dad's one looked about two sizes too small. I watched them jog down the road then I jogged to the door, at least I'd get Debbie alone!

As I rang the doorbell an image of Debbie in P.E. kit jumped into my mind. Made my mouth water.

"Hello, Greg."

No P.E. kit I'm afraid, but she looked fairly stunning all the same. And she was smiling. "Come in."

"Came round earlier but you and your family were . . ."

"Family conference. I'm in the kitchen, by the way."

I followed her into a large and disgustingly clean kitchen. "My turn to wash up."

"Was that what the family conference was about?" I joked.

But Debbie answered me seriously. "No, we have a rota for that." She pointed to a chart above the sink. "No, this was about pocket money. Alistair put in for a 10% pay increase. So did I. We got a 7% rise."

"Great. Want a hand?"

"Yes." She handed me the brush. "You wash, I'll dry and put away. Do you want an apron?"

"Definitely not."

She laughed. "Think it would ruin your image. You've got a bad reputation, you know." She said it teasingly. "Hear you dump girls after about two dates."

"Some don't last that long."

"I wonder how long I'd last."

It was becoming harder to steady my voice. "Quite a long time. Perhaps forever." I banged a dish down so I didn't think she heard the last two words.

But she did hear. "Oh, how sweet."

"I'll take you to the party on Friday, if you like." The words ripped out.

"Yes, I would like." She put the dish cloth down and kissed me. The brush bounded out of my arms and fell onto a large jug. I held her close and half closed my eyes. A dream was coming true.

With her first kiss came a brief, but sharp charge of pain. Always get it during a good kiss. Then her tongue plunged into my mouth again; this time a thousand volts of ecstasy shot through me.

The kiss never ended it just grew, suddenly Debbie's lips were on my neck and her hands were skimming downwards, deftly undoing the buttons on my shirt. Then she pulled and tugged at my shirt. "It won't come," she whispered.

"I will, though."

She half laughed, half gasped, then she took the shirt off my shoulders. Very gently she rubbed one shoulder, then the other. Then her hands travelled down my body . . .

further and further. She sighed or did I? Her finger slid into my belly button just as a key slid through a lock.

Debbie jumped away from me as if she'd received a massive electric shock. I was still reeling and dreaming. "Put your shirt on. Quick," she cried. She closed the kitchen door as her family spewed in through the front door.

I could hear her father shouting, "I'm all right. I'm all right. Just sprained my ankle."

The kitchen door opened. I was still tucking in my shirt. No one noticed. All were concentrating on Debbie's dad wobbling to a seat.

"Greg is helping with the washing up," said Debbie over casually.

"Got you working, has she?" said her mum.

Her dad gave me a nod. "Excuse my unsteady entrance," he said, sinking into a chair.

I wonder if he'd have excused the scene that had taken place between Debbie and me. I wonder what would have happened if her family hadn't returned . . .

Two hours later I soared home. Debbie and I didn't have any more time alone, we looked at photo albums and home movies of Debbie but always with one or more of the family in attendance.

Didn't matter. Nothing could dilute the memory of our embrace. And now I knew for sure that Debbie fancied me – no more than that. I stirred up her hormones, she stirred up mine. My hormones were still shook up, and she hadn't mentioned Gaz all evening – not once.

I almost sailed past Andy, who was slouched against my front wall. He jumped out of the shadows. "Where've you been?"

"Out."

"Not been round Gaz's bird's again?"

"No, been round Debbie's house. And now I'm going to bed. I'm knackered."

"Bet you are. Any good is she?"

"Dynamite."

I walked up my steps.

"You know what happens when you play with dynamite, don't you," called Andy. "You get blown up."

"Piss off, Andy," I said.

His tone changed. "Listen to a mate. You're heading for trouble if you try to nestle in between Gaz and his bird."

I wheeled round. "They chucked each other."

"Good for Gaz. So why do you want to bother with that stuck up cow with a chin you can ski off."

"Listen, Andy, and listen well. I like Debbie. And we're going to Jo's party tomorrow. We're going together." I was really spelling it out now. "Also, you've never had a steady girlfriend so where do you get off giving me advice?"

That was a bit below the belt. Andy slunk down my drive, spitting onto the daffodils as he said, "Good luck, mate. You're going to need it." He didn't wait for an answer.

Jealous – that's what Andy is. Just wait till Andy sees what's going to happen on Friday. In anticipation of Friday, I even scribbled CANCELLED over his GAZ FOR DEBBIE heart on Smokers' Wall. Bit kiddish – but on Monday I'll write GREG FOR DEBBIE. No, I'll write GREG FOR DEBS.

First though, I've got one more job to do.

Log / Day Seven / Thursday

If you saw me now you'd think I had a hangover. You'd be right. All in a good cause, though. You see I've just got back from Gaz's.

Rang him after school. Wanted to tell him I was taking Debs to the party tomorrow and how I felt about her – well, hint about how I felt – as well as try to persuade him not to go. Anyway, Gaz says he's babysitting for his dad and step-mum and why don't I go round.

I actually wrote down headings to remind me what I was going to say to him. Even had one heading: CARE. That was to remind me to say, "I really care about Debs and I promise I will look after her." Yuk!!

Found Gaz cracking into a bottle of home-made wine. His dad's a great wine-maker. Gaz says it's the only interest he and his dad have in common. So even before I sat down I got this pint glass of wine in my hand. It smelt awful, looked awful and by golly it was awful. Like medicine. Really bitter.

But Gaz was downing it – so I thought I'd better. In fact, Gaz acted as if he was doing an Andy impression saying, "Get the hooch down you", and topping me up every four seconds. Never seen Gaz like this before.

Mind you, I've never been so hyped up either. It was as if I was about to take part in a race and was straining on the touch-line, impatient for the starting pistol. I kept walking about pretending to look at pictures I'd seen hundreds of times before – felt steadier on my feet. Then, suddenly, as if a pistol had gone off in my head, I was off. "Went round Debs again last night."

"I know, stayed a couple of hours or was it even longer?"

How did he always know. "No, about two hours. Saw all her modelling pictures and tons of snapshots."

He became thoughtful. "Debs is the only girl I know whose eyes never go red in pictures. Did you know that?" Gaz didn't wait for my answer. "Me, my eyes often look red. But her – she can stand right by the flash and her eyes still come out perfect. Good trick – don't know how she does it. But then she's full of tricks, isn't she?"

Suddenly he was peering at me.

"Yeah, yeah. Talking of tricks, thought her family were doing a trick when I arrived yesterday. Saw them all sitting round the table and . . ."

"Family conference," interrupted Gaz. "They're always having family conferences. They discuss everything. Were they discussing me yesterday?"

"Debs said it was pocket money."

"It was me. Her dad's never liked me. I mean, he'd be all smiles to my face but I knew. I knew. Have some more hooch?"

"No, I'm okay."

"Have some more hooch. No, they were discussing me. Bet her dad celebrated last night with me out of the scene. Now his dear daughter can go out with a real man – one with a car, a house, two yachts."

"Only two?"

"Okay four. And a degree. Degree in Latin."

"And Greek."

"Of course!" Gaz sat back as if he could see the family conference on the wall. "They'd discuss me and Lizzie, too. All the lies. Why won't she believe me, Jugger?"

"Er, well, perhaps she's doing you a favour. Giving you a chance to go out with some different girls . . ."

Gaz pointed his finger at me as if he was a teacher. "Don't get me wrong, Jugger. I want to split with her. I really do. But I want her to know the truth – and then break with her. And the laugh will be on her, won't it? If I could only get to her and tell her so she'd listen."

"Yeah, if only," I said faintly.

"I've got it," said Gaz. He stood up now. "Yeah – that's it. Come on, drink to my idea."

"What is your idea?"

"I'll have Debs attacked on the road, the Penn Road, by these bandits, really ruthless, cut-your-head-off-if-you-sneeze bandits. Then I will come charging round the corner on a white horse . . ."

"A palamino," I volunteered, anxious to keep Gaz in this silly frame of mind.

"Yeah, a palamino, and I'll carry her off to the Octagon

83

and she'll be so grateful she'll be hanging on my neck smothering it with kisses, and then I'll tell her the truth about Friday night and she'll say 'Gaz, I'm so sorry' but I'll just say 'Push off you bitch' and . . ."

"Shove her off the palamino."

"That's it. No, that's too simple."

I picked up his mood. "What about training a squad of killer wasps to buzz through her window – during one of the family conferences – then they overpower her and she's lying on the floor . . ."

"Let me finish it," said Gaz, all excited. "And I happen to be passing, hear all that buzzing, think for a moment, is that her dad, and then I hear her screaming and I think, funny. Are the wasps turning her on with their deadly stings. So I burst through the glass."

"Aren't you hurt?"

"No, got my special glass protection vest and face mask on."

"Wearing it now?"

"Yeah."

"Bet you're really good-looking without the mask?"

Gaz jumps onto my chair and sits on my head. With me squashed, he continues, "Then I fight off the one zillion wasps, but guess what?"

"What?"

"As I fight off the last wasp, Debs sinks to the ground, chin first."

"That's cruel."

"Shut up. And she cries 'Save me' but it's too late. The wasps have given her a rare blood disease – only one person has the same type of blood as her. Yes, hunky me. So I offer my blood on one condition. You know what that is?"

"That she listens to your version of Friday night."

"She listens to the truth about Friday night."

"And does she?"

"Oh yeah. And she sobs, sobs buckets. And then I say,

'Now here's something to really get your taps going. I'm not donating the blood after all. Ha, Ha, Ha.' She laughs too, thinking I'm joking. In fact she dies, laughing. What do you think?"

"Just one thing."

"Yeah?"

"Could you please get off my head now."

"Just as I was getting comfortable." Gaz wriggled up.

"Ow, you're heavy," I said rubbing my head.

"Got just the cure." Gaz shot off into the kitchen and started laughing really maniacally, as if he was playing Count Dracula in one of those old horror movies. Then he comes back with a sponge. "Catch," he says. It lands right on my face. It's soaking.

Soon a major water fight is in progress. It begins with wet cloths but quickly advances to mugs of water thrown in the kitchen. Then Gaz fills this tankard, shouts, "Jugger, I give in," and as I sneak my head round the door he shouts, "No, I don't," and directs the jug's contents at me – only I duck – and instead it sprays all over the wallpaper. This mini-waterfall springs up as Rosalyn, one of the dingoes we're babysitting for, comes in crying, "You're making too much noise." Then she sees the water sliding down the wall, examines it and coos, "Oh, Gary, you are really in trouble now. When my mum comes back – you're going to get it."

But it's Rosalyn who gets it: a soggy blue cloth right on her neck, she pushes it off as if it's an insect.

"First time water's ever touched her neck," quips Gaz.

Rosalyn, furious, continues to hurl nasties. "My big half brother – who behaves like a little kid. No wonder Deborah left you. Wonder she stuck you so long."

"Watch it, you squint-eyed runt," said Gaz. "I'm in just the mood to beat you up."

He advanced on her. She retreated to the door. "I'm going. Don't want to stay here." She did a little madam flounce and flung one final nastie. "Bet my mum kills you for doing that. You know you've stained the wall for ever."

As soon as she swayed off Gaz began studying the water stains. "Wall doesn't look too bad."

"I think it's an improvement. No, it'll dry out. I'm going to make us both coffee. Anything but that wine."

"I'll do it." He tapped the stains. "Drying already."

"Don't know if I will, though," I said, filling the kettle. "I'm soaked."

"So am I. Look at my trousers. Looks like I've wet myself. Did at school once. There was this big puddle under my table."

"How long ago did that happen?"

"Only last week." Gaz smiled. "Debs is good in water fights."

"Well, she doesn't like getting hit. She thought she should just be allowed to throw water. Good shot, too. That surprises you?"

"It does. I suppose I thought she was above that sort of thing." I turned to plug in the kettle.

"Nah, Debs acts grand but really she's quite ordinary. I know it. She doesn't have to act with me. That's why we get along. Or did." He suddenly turned on me. "You like Debs, don't you?"

I felt winded. Hadn't expected that comment so suddenly, so casually. Now was my chance to tell the truth, set the record straight. So what did I do? I changed the subject. "She's okay. She's going to Jo Martin's party tomorrow. Don't suppose you will?"

Gaz didn't answer. He squelched down on the floor – which currently resembled a swamp. "Sit down a minute."

I sat down.

"You think I should go?"

"Well, er . . ."

"Okay, I'll go. I'm taking that girl, Lizzie Something."

"The girl from last Friday?" I was amazed and delighted.

86

"Yeah, that girl Lizzie Smith or Lizzie Jones or Lizzie Sixtoes . . . whatever she's called."

"Didn't know you'd asked her."

"Haven't yet."

"But you like her?"

"Is she the one with blonde hair and the quite big. . . ?"

"Yeah."

"I like her."

"Do you know where she lives?" I was egging him on.

He turned over onto his back and started kicking his legs out. "I think she lives in a sewer." he muttered.

"Which sewer?"

"Don't know. I'll go and sniff her out, shall I?" He eased himself up as if he was clambering out of thick mud.

But now it was time to stop being silly. I really wanted Gaz to renew his acquaintance with Lizzie whoever. "Rubi will know her other name."

Gaz shook himself, spraying water over me. "Good thinking, Batman, I'll give Rubi a ring now." He ran into the dining room then ran back again, giggling. "What's Rubi's number?"

"It's in the book. Here, you pour out the coffee, I'll find it."

Guilt swept over me as I hunted out Rubi's phone number. I was trying to fix Gaz up with a girl he hardly remembered – while I swiped his girlfriend. I was pretending to aid Gaz, giving him a new girl to care about, a girl to help him forget Debs etc., but really what I was doing, to borrow Andy's phrase, was playing with dynamite. For if Debs saw Gaz with Lizzie that would be it. Gaz's relationship with Debs would expire for ever. I knew that and yet . . .

I dialled Rubi's number. Wrote down Lizzie's number and name (Turner) and rang Lizzie's number. Then I gave Gaz the phone.

Talking to Lizzie seemed to sober Gaz up a bit. He was

very nice, actually, spoke as if he was dead keen on her. Perhaps I'd brainwashed him into thinking he fancied Lizzie.

When Gaz banged the phone down he was smiling. "In the bag, mate. She said she was going out with the girls to some club tomorrow but she'd see if she could get out of it."

I had a strong feeling Lizzie would get out of it. Girls seem to like Gaz. I mean, genuinely like Gaz. Perhaps because he's a bit lost, bit unhappy (misses his mum a lot more than he lets on), but is really a decent guy. And a laugh.

Just as I was leaving, Gaz suddenly says to me, "That girl I rang up. What was her name?"

"Turner."

"No, her first name."

I winced. What had I got Gaz into. Last Friday, one of his best mates, Andy, set him up (certainly spiked his drinks anyhow) and now a week later I was setting Gaz up. But at least it was all in a good cause. Who knows, one evening we might go out as a foursome. Gaz and Lizzie and Debs and me. Debs and me – by the end of tomorrow night we could be what they call an "item", if I can only pull it off!!

Log / Day Eight / Friday

I'll just give you the facts. They are these:

Called for Debs at exactly eight o'clock. Of course, she kept me waiting. I expected that. So I waited in the kitchen where I shook hands with her dad (he seemed to have forgotten he'd met me only two days earlier), and stroked just about every hair of their spaniel – anything to cover up my nervousness.

Debs appeared at nearly nine o'clock, dress shiny and glittery and sexy, she looked as if she'd been sprayed into it.

Debs chattered loudly, amusingly and feverishly all the way to Jo's house. Then we set our faces into our "I'm cool but enjoying myself" look and chatted loudly and vaguely with a strange assortment of 5th and 6th years, and "weren't you down the village hall two years ago" people.

No one seemed in the slightest relaxed. Debs appeared distinctly flushed – even though she kept laughing loudly at jokes she couldn't possibly have heard.

Every so often she'd whisper to me, "All right", which was nice. Would have been nicer if she'd actually looked at me when she said it – or waited for my answer. Instead her eyes were darting around the room searching out . . .

He arrived at one minute to ten. Know that because I was looking at my watch when I caught the sound of her in-drawn breath, felt her suddenly squeeze my hand tight and whisper, "All right".

Was it my imagination or did the room actually freeze as Gaz made his way through the crowd, arm in arm with Lizzie Turner, to the drinks table. I certainly noticed how a small crowd was circling round us, not actually talking to us just watching. Same thing was happening at the opposite end . . . with Gaz and Lizzie being the objects to stare at, nudge and whisper about.

"Do you want to go into the kitchen?" I asked Debs.

"No, no, quite happy."

"See Gaz has arrived."

"Has he? Oh yes. Is that the girl who . . ."

"Yes, that's Lizzie Turner."

"Looks what she is – the sort who lets a man put his hand up her dress after two minutes."

"Goes to the high school."

"They're the worst. Sex starved. Anything in trousers."

"Still Gaz seems to really like her," I added. "I think it could be serious."

Debs sounded as if she was choking, then she started laughing. "I think I'm a bit tight already."

"But you've only had an orange juice."

"Well, I feel tight." Then her eyes went to . . . She couldn't stop watching Gaz and Lizzie. They weren't doing anything worth watching really. Just talking rather half-heartedly. But Debs's eyes were on them. She was beginning to annoy me.

Wildly now, "Hear Gaz has asked Lizzie out."

"Good! Good!" said Debs.

"I think Lizzie has accepted too."

"Poor girl. Still, look at her, caked in make-up. High school girls always put on too much lipstick, she looks like a clown."

"Yet Gaz likes her, just as I like you."

"How disgusting."

"What?" But Debs wasn't even listening to me, she was watching Gaz stroking Lizzie's arm.

"Look at him," she said.

"He's only touching her arm," I replied.

"No, no, I can see right through him."

"Not surprised. Been looking at him long enough."

Instantly I wished I hadn't said that. But I had said it and Debs heard me. "Excuse me," she said frostily.

"Debs. I . . ."

But she departed, obviously to find Jo or some other ally. And I'd ruined it all. Of course she was bound to stare at Gaz with another girl. Be strange for her at first. But if I'd given her a bit of time she'd have got used to it.

Across the room I heard Lizzie call, "Won't be a minute, Gaz," as she skipped off, presumably to the loo.

Gaz came over.

"Having a good time?" I said.

"Brilliant."

"Lizzie looks good."

"Doesn't she though."

"Seems a nice person, too."

"One of the best."

Silence, then . . . "Could you do me a favour, Jugger?"

"Sure."

"See her home for me."

"What?"

Gaz shushed me. "I'm not feeling too good. So I'm going home right now."

"But you've only just arrived. Besides, what about Lizzie?"

"She'll be all right."

"Won't she be out of things?"

"Lizzie knows a few people. I'd count it as a real favour. Goodnight mate."

I stared after him, open-mouthed, too astonished to argue. But how could I see both Lizzie and Debs home. Providing Debs was still talking to me. Providing Debs hadn't gone home yet.

However, I soon realized that Debs was still at the party. Didn't see her, heard her, well I heard someone yell, "Fight, Fight", and saw, rolling around on the landing floor, Debs and Lizzie. Debs was pulling at Lizzie's hair, while Lizzie seemed to be trying to pull at Debs earrings. "Go for the neck," yelled someone. But Debs didn't need any advice (if the advice was for her, which I doubt) for suddenly her nails popped out and she started scratching Lizzie's face.

Meanwhile, Jo is screaming at Debs to "stop, stop!" while the crowd is screaming encouragement, and suddenly Andy is pushing his way through the crowd, calling, "Gangway, gangway". He has a large bucket in his hand and tips the contents over the fighting girls.

Then . . . I went outside into the garden for about half an hour. No one else about. All inside talking about the fight, endlessly replaying each action-packed moment.

Me. I wanted to forget it.

Don't know how long I was in the garden. Quite a long time, anyhow, before I went back inside. Didn't like what Debbie had done, fighting and all, but I had brought her here, so it was my duty to see her home. And, anyway, it was all my fault. I'd persuaded Gaz, when he was in a very low state of mind, to bring Lizzie. I thought of the result. Gaz so upset he leaves a party after twenty minutes, Debs and Lizzie both battle scarred. For once, Andy was right. I had been playing with dynamite.

I went back inside. Stairs now cleared, the party crammed into Jo's lounge and kitchen, all seemed more at ease. Nothing like a good fight for relaxing everyone.

However, neither Debbie nor Lizzie seemed to be about. Don't tell me they were having a good heart to heart upstairs.

I found Jo, ferrying food about in the kitchen. "Where's Debbie?" I said.

"Upstairs," she began.

I rushed upstairs, was about to knock on Jo's bedroom door when I heard what sounded like a slap. Two, three quite hearty slaps. Surely Debbie and Lizzie couldn't be . . . but then I heard Debbie laughing. A proper laugh. And then I heard another laugh. Gaz's laugh.

Next there was some whispering, a lot of whispering and then a silence. I believe I was ear-wigging on a process called making up. I listened some more. The whispers became harder to decipher but I could translate – everyone knows what the language of love sounds like. I listened long and hard. This was the nearest I'd get to Debbie's expressions of love. I knew that, now.

I thought I'd been so clever with my little games and deceptions but they were playing games too. Though not deliberately. And all that stuff Debbie told me about Gaz farting and having smelly feet, it was probably all true. And all irrelevant.

Just like Lizzie and me were irrelevant to them. We were just counters, to be moved about so they could eventually reach their destination. Tonight, thanks to me, Gaz and Debbie (never Debs) were back where they belonged. Together.

"Isn't it good they're back together again," said Jo.

I hadn't heard her creeping up the stairs. "Wonderful."

"When Gaz heard about the fight he tore over."

"Can imagine. Any cuts or bruises on either of the wrestlers?"

"Not a mark on Debbie. Typical, isn't it. Poor Lizzie's got a few scratches – but mainly I think it was the shock. You see, it was so sudden. I mean, one minute Debbie is up here, just as calm as can be – nodding and smiling at everyone, then she spots Lizzie coming out of the loo and pow . . ."

"Never know what people really think and feel, do you?" I said. "Spend most of our lives keeping it all bottled up."

Jo looked at me curiously. Same way she'd looked at me when I went round to her house on Sunday. It unnerved me. "So where's Lizzie now?" I asked.

"Gone home, Rubi took her."

"Well, I'm off home, too."

"You're not going in to see Gaz and Debbie."

It was hearing that phrase "Gaz and Debbie" that set me off. I felt tears pricking my eyes and I could hardly speak, perhaps because I had a lump in my throat the size of a golf ball. So I just stuttered, "Goodbye", at Jo and shot down stairs.

Heard her say, "Don't go, Greg, stay a while."

Had she guessed that I loved Debbie? Was she feeling sorry for me. That thought made me run all the way home.

And now – now, it's 2.00 a.m. Never wanted to write my log tonight. But I had no choice. For when I lay down and tried to sleep I had this weird sensation; something, something I couldn't see, was pressing down hard on me, trying to smother me. I'd call it a nightmare only I was awake. But it was as real as any nightmare.

I sat up, shaking and gasping, bunged the lights on in my room and the landing – and to steady myself, started writing.

Also been re-reading this log. Don't recognize myself.

But then, haven't been myself – not since last Friday. That's when Debbie got me in her grip – and she's got a strong grip. Right now she's holding me in a half-nelson right across my heart.

No. That's self-pitying crap. Can't blame Debbie. Only me. Gonna try to sleep again, this time sitting up with the light on. Anything's better than lying here aching. This is even worse than toothache. For you can't do anything to stop this pain going on . . . and probably on and on. Unlike this journal. I, hereby end it. I've bled enough words.

P.S.

One last thing: underneath my final entry I'd written in huge green capitals: "LOVE: Something you feel for a dog or a pussy cat."

A quote, courtesy of Johnny Rotten, courtesy of Smash Hits. For a while tried to pretend I believed that quote.

But then I hadn't been in LOVE with Debbie, had I? It had just been a crush, a phase, an adolescent attack of lust – I don't know. All I know, it made me ache for weeks.

Anyway, let's make war – not love. Next story is a bit nasty. Things got pretty hairy when war broke out in the Hazlemere estate. Andy's involved in the battle – you guessed that.

Okay – let's parachute over the page to . . .

Chicken War Begins Tonight

"You want trouble, mate, you got it," said Andy.

Before the guy could reply, Andy had landed him one, right at the side of his beaky nose. Andy left an impression on that guy's cheek and the rest of the pub, which lasted all night. Just what Andy had intended.

I never saw this guy giving Andy a bad eye. But according to Andy every bloke hates him on sight. Saves time, I suppose.

Andy's always trying to prove how hard he is. Except when girls are around. Then he goes all pratty. Like when we went swimming once. And these girls were looking at us. So Andy starts prancing about, behaving really kiddish, feeling his muscles and all – until one girl calls out loudly, "What a prick!"

"Didn't know it was that obvious," Andy calls back.

But I think he knew what she really meant.

Behind Andy's back most people reckon he's a prick. Except me. I like him. But he can be a real dick-head. Like the time he caused a war, the "Chicken War". I'm sure you've played Chicken. Two lads (with a capital L) stand opposite each other, legs really wide apart. Then you throw the darts between the guys' legs. Easy. But after each throw the legs get closer together until finally it gets pretty risky, especially if you're playing Andy. He's a very wide thrower.

No one wants to play Chicken with Andy. Except Asaf Latif. And even he wasn't keen at first. Who is Asaf Latif? A crucial figure in the war, that's who. He's known to his enemies (he hasn't got any friends) as Giblet. He's at Garson School, the other local secondary, only he's been suspended, to quote Giblet, "for sticking two fingers up a teacher", and now he was sampling the delights of Farndale School, behind the bike sheds at break-time. And being treated as a bit of a hero, which narked Andy.

So Andy suddenly goes, "What about a game of chicken, Giblet?"

"No," Giblet tries to turn away.

"Bottler!"

"No!" Giblet was getting mad.

"Give me a game, then." Andy widened his legs, looking down below. "I've got more to lose than you."

All eyes were on Giblet. His new-found respect was ebbing away.

"I'll play Chicken with you, Horny, but we'll play it Garson way."

"You mean the girlie way," sneered Andy.

"No, no, follow me." Giblet walked around the school, looking in at the classrooms. Then he stopped outside Bryne's cave. "This one is just right," he said.

He backed off the path onto the edge of the field. "We stand here, legs apart, all right? Now, you see that wood there?" He pointed to a window frame opposite. "You gotta throw the darts through your own legs onto the wood. Like so."

He performed a perfect throw, landing the dart right in the centre of the wood.

"Easy," said Andy.

"No, I made it look easy," corrected Giblet.

Andy snatched the dart away, and did his usual wide throw. His dart landed about a mile short of the target.

"You've been practising." Giblet's sarky comment got some laughs from the swelling crowd.

Andy flushed. He was getting mad.

"I'll show you again. Now watch," taunted Giblet

I'll show you my first in a minute muttered Andy.

Giblet drew his legs closer together, called out, "Here we go, boys", and performed another excellent throw.

Andy glared at the audience who clapped Giblet, then grabbed the dart out of the wood.

"Remember you aim at the wood – not the umbrella you aimed at before," sneered Giblet.

An old umbrella lay on the path. Been there for days. Andy'd nearly hit it last time. Now he picked the umbrella up. I thought he was going to throw it at Giblet. Giblet thought so too. He ducked when Andy started waving it above his head. But instead, Andy tossed the old umbrella onto the field and said, all keyed up, "Now you'll see something."

He deliberately placed his legs closer together than Giblet's had been, then he made a low whistling noise and whispered "Shot" – just before the dart flew straight onto the glass. BANG!

There was one minute's silence as everyone stared, open-mouthed, at the crack which started in one area of the glass, then grew and grew. The glass didn't fall out, just stayed there all frosted. Finally, Andy picked up the dart and shouted, "Everyone scarper."

But it was too late. For striding up the path was Bryne. He yelled, "Stop, right there."

"This is your Life," murmured Gaz to me.

"No, This is your Death," I murmured back, actually feeling a bit sorry for Andy.

"Andrew Horne, did you break that window?"

"Yes, sir." When in trouble, call a teacher "sir". Always softens them up.

"Do you know how much that window will cost to repair?"

"No."

"A hundred pounds. Have you got a hundred pounds?"

"No."

"And do you . . ." Byrne paused. He noticed someone out of uniform trying to melt away. "You boy. What are you doing here?"

Gilbert looked blank.

"Do you know you're trespassing!"

Giblet continued his sleep-walking act.

"Did you invite this boy here?" Byrne turned back to Andy.

Andy nodded, "Yes."

"Why? You know it's illegal."

Andy gazed around him for inspiration. He found it on the back field. "He was bringing my umbrella back."

"Your umbrella?"

"Yes, he borrowed it last night." Andy held up the very dirty, very ancient umbrella.

Bryne wrinkled his nose in distaste. "You're telling me this boy arrived here to bring you that disgusting umbrella?"

"Yes, yes," said Giblet, suddenly finding his voice. "I said, 'Andy, here's your umbrella.' He said, 'Throw it to me.' I did. And as you can see, he missed the catch." Giblet couldn't resist grinning after that last sentence.

Andy grunted. He didn't like that story. But it was better than the truth.

Bryne looked at Giblet curiously. "Why aren't you at school?" he said.

"On holiday," said Giblet quickly.

"In February?"

"Asian custom," said Giblet again.

But Bryne suddenly became very excited and started giving Giblet strange looks. "Well, I think both of you should go to the Headmaster and tell him your story right now. Come on! Come on!"

Normally Bryne only gets this excited when the bell goes for break-time. It did seem a bit O.T.T. to send them both to Moggie for a broken window. Even one worth a hundred pounds. But Bryne was really pushing them towards the torture chamber.

For what happens next I'm reliant on Andy. He says that

he and Giblet were marched outside Moggie's pad. Bryne goes, "Wait here", and runs into Moggie's room.

Of course, Bryne in his excitement forgets Giblet isn't a pupil and as soon as Bryne disappears, so does Giblet — legging it out of the school in about ten seconds. And who could blame him.

Then Bryne comes out, fairly shrieking, "Where's the Asian boy?"

"Gone," says Andy, enjoying Bryne's discomfort.

Bryne staggers into Moggie's office and, a few seconds later, totters out. "I'll get him," he mutters, then said, almost as an afterthought, "Go in, Horne."

God wasn't in a good mood. A watering can lay on his desk. He'd been interrupted.

"I think you'd better apologize, hadn't you?" said Moggie.

"Sorry, sir."

"Not to me, you fool, to my plants. Their vital watering time has been disturbed while I have to deal with you."

"Oh."

"Well, apologize then."

"Sorry, plants," whispered Andy.

"Louder."

"Sorry, plants," he shouted.

"It's very difficult for plants to grow in an unpleasant polluted atmosphere. Why do you pollute my atmosphere?"

Andy didn't even bother to answer that one.

"Sit."

Andy sat down.

"What made you think I was talking to you. I could be talking to my dog."

Andy stood up again.

"But I haven't got a dog. So you know I meant you. Use your commonsense, lad."

Andy sat down, wondering if all headmasters were as mental as this one.

"Broken a window, haven't you?" said Moggie.

Andy nodded.

"Do you know how much glass costs to repair?"

"A hundred pounds."

Moggie laughed bitterly. "Ha, those windows have been specially imported from Scotland. Be lucky if you get away with – a thousand pounds."

Andy was stunned. There's no way his family would pay that.

"Surprised you, haven't I? Taken the wind out of your sails?" Moggie's boot-black eyes bored into Andy. "Got a thousand pounds, have you?"

Andy shivered.

"Want a cigarette?"

Andy shivered once more. Especially when Moggie produced a packet of ciggies. "Go on, have one." It was almost an order.

Andy took one. Moggie produced a lighter. Andy puffed nervously at his cigarette.

"You've had a shock," said Moggie smoothly. "Thousand pounds is a lot of money. Still, it wasn't really your fault. Asaf threw the umbrella, didn't he?"

"Yes. But I told him to. It was my fault."

Moggie shot up in his chair. "So it was Asaf Latif who was here."

Too late, Andy realized the trap he'd fallen into. Moggie was already on the phone. "Get me Garson School." He glared at Andy. "There was a case conference about Latif yesterday. Mr Byrne attended – only Asaf Latif didn't turn up. Parents said he'd gone away to relatives. Luckily, Mr Bryne thought he recognized him . . . thank you for confirming." His tone changed. "And put that cigarette out. A letter is going home to your parents about the broken window and your smoking. In front of my plants too . . ."

That's Andy's story. And I believe him. He'd never grass any one up, not even Giblet. It was Bryne, thinking he'd get his teacher stripe for sighting bad boy Giblet that did the grassing. But of course, when Giblet gets picked up at his home later that day, guess who he blamed.

Next day Andy was not a happy man. Reckon his dad had taken a belt to him for Andy sat down and got up really carefully. And Andy's dad is savage. Remember once he was picking us up from a rock concert. It had over-run as concerts often do but before Andy could explain, his dad hit him across the face. Wham! "Don't ever keep me waiting again," he yelled.

Whenever Andy narks me I try to think of his dad.

But Andy didn't speak about what his dad had done to him – he just sat there, eyes glazed, fist clenched. The teacher who was covering for Bryne (he was at guess whose case conference) gave Andy a very wide berth.

And as soon as the bell went for lunch Andy leapt out. He even had some ciggies of his own (first time ever) and he tore over to Smokers' Wall, ahead of everyone else. Well, almost everyone else.

One person was busy writing a new piece of graffiti DEATH TO GRASSER HOR . . . Never got a chance to add the NE. I mean it's a bit difficult to paint when someone's pressing his very big hand against your throat. All you can do is choke. Which is what Giblet was doing. Loudly.

By the time we tore over Giblet was turning blue.

"Let him go, Andy," I said.

"Did you see what he wrote?" said Andy.

We all looked at the offending graffiti.

"That's well out of order but you're killing him, Andy," warned Gaz.

Giblet wasn't even choking any more. Andy didn't seem bothered.

"And he's half your size," I said.

Andy released him. Giblet fell on to the ground gasping for breath. Then he whispered, "You grasser."

"He didn't grass on you," I said. "Andy wouldn't do that."

"Oh, you would say that," snarled Giblet. "When I told my family what Horne had done they were as mad as me. They drove me over here after that . . . that thing you put me through this morning. And they said, 'Tell everyone the truth about the boy who told on you' . . . and my family . . ."

"Your family," yelled Andy. "What, all twenty-nine of them. How many of them are asleep now. You know, their house is so crowded they have to sleep in shifts."

"Not true. Not true," said Giblet, angry tears stinging his eyes.

"Go back to your own country," yelled Andy. "We don't want you or your poxy music, do we, lads?"

Up to now we'd been backing Andy up. We knew he wasn't a grasser. But now he was going loony. Both he and Giblet were.

"I'll get you. I'll get you," said Giblet. "I'll be back with some mates bigger than you."

"Bring all the jungle bunnies you want. There's enough of them at your blackie school. We'll be waiting, won't we, lads?"

Our "Yeahs" were growing fainter. Gaz looked furious.

Then Andy took the paint brush and scrawled over DEATH TO GRASSER HOR . . . CHICKEN WAR BEGINS AFTER SCHOOL. He threw the paint brush at Giblet, missing as usual. However, Giblet spluttered as if the brush had hit him, calling "Just you wait. Just you wait." Then he darted away, yelling things way into the distance. Andy was yelling too. "Bring the whole school if you want. We'll be ready won't we?" But no one backed him up.

Most of the lads were angry with Andy but it was Denise who dared voice what we were thinking. "Why do you always have to shoot your mouth off?"

Andy looked stunned. He was always ill at ease with girls. "He called me a grasser," he muttered.

"Okay, but that's no reason for you to give him all that racist crap."

"It's not crap."

"I think it's crap and I bet most of the people here agree. And I'll tell you something else, I'm not getting into some battle with another school – just 'cause you got a big mouth."

"Neither am I," said Jo.

There were murmurs of agreement from the other girls.

"We'll take 'em on, won't we, lads?"

"I thought you spoke a load of balls," said Gaz quietly.

"So did I," said Phil.

Everyone, brave now, backed Gaz and Phil up. I didn't say anything. I agreed with Gaz – but Andy was my best mate.

Andy started laughing really loudly and falsley. "Yellow, the lot of you. Well I'm not frightened by Giblet or any of his bum-chums."

"How many bum-chums do you reckon there'll be?" I asked.

"Three, four at the most," said Andy. "But if that turd wants hassle, I'll give him hassle." He smacked his fists together. The he laughed again. No one else did.

Last two lessons up in the lecture theatre: even I was getting mad at Andy by now. For I'd just been having a joke with Gaz when Andy has to bomb over forcing his way in between us. "What's the gag, lads. Laughing at me, were you?"

I didn't even bother to answer him. I knew Andy was getting juiced up but did he have to be such a pain as well? A big anit-Andy movement was growing – until 3.44. That was when Gaz let out a small, sharp cry. Ten seconds later he let out a larger cry. Soon the whole class joined Gaz, looking out of the window and gave their own cries of shock and horror, at the sight of . . .

Estimates vary as to how many there were. There weren't a hundred, probably no more than forty, but each one of the forty looked mean, vicious and – tooled up. One guy was brandishing a block of wood. Denise claimed she could see nails in it. I'm sure I spotted a knife or two and . . . I stopped looking.

"Look at 'em all," said Rubi. "I know that one, he's called Naseem, Naseem Khan, supposed to be the hardest guy around and that one . . ."

"Rubi, shut up," said Andy.

"Oh, that's fine coming from you," cried Denise. "If you'd shut up none of this would be happening."

"Andy can't take on all that lot alone, can he?" I said, trying to alter the tone of the conversation.

"Yes he can," said Denise. "They've just come for Andy."

"Are you sure?" asked Gaz.

No one answered his question. It just hung there in the air. While the Garson army disappeared from view.

"They'll be waiting outside the school. What'll we do?" asked Rubi.

"I'll just blow 'em away," said Andy, still trying to act The Man.

"I bet we're surrounded," said Debbie dramatically. "There'll be a massacre."

"I never saw Giblet," said Rubi suddenly.

"He probably went on ahead," said Gaz.

"No, I bet he's crawled up someone's leg, he's so little," snarled Andy. But he was squinting his brown eyes, doing his piggy look, sure sign he was worried. "Just keep calm," he finished.

"Hark who's talking," snorted Denise.

Any more conversation was cut short by the bell. The bell! Never had it sounded less welcome. For the first time in the history of the universe, pupils heard the bell and didn't move.

Avery, our Physics teacher, popped out of the lab assistant's office (he'd been giving her private lessons) and said, "Go on, off you go. You can finish copying up next week. Well go on, then. You don't normally need telling twice."

The lab assistant coughed. A "don't keep me waiting" cough. "Off you go," repeated Avery impatiently.

For a mad second I thought of telling Avery about the assailants waiting outside. But no, I couldn't do that. Besides, Avery had closed his door very firmly. He didn't want to be disturbed.

"Everyone follow me," said Andy.

We followed him, we're used to following Andy. Especially in a crisis, even if it was a crisis Andy had caused.

"We'll leave in force," said Andy. "Won't dare touch us then. I'll go in front," he added.

We all jostled down to the cloakroom, wrapping coats around us especially carefully.

"Don't go out alone," Andy warned the younger kids there.

"Why not?"

"A few jungle-bunnies waiting outside."

"I'm what you would call a jungle-bunny," piped up one Indian boy.

"No, you're not – because you go to this school. Anyway, I'm going out first, advise you to follow behind me. Spread the word."

The word spread. Soon the cloakroom was clogged up with little kids buzzing with excitement – and terror. Andy raised his hand for silence. "Remember, keep in your groups and follow behind my group."

"Yes, Andy," said the kids.

"Look at him," whispered Denise, "doing the big 'I am' act to those kids. They think he's great."

In an awful sort of way Andy was great as he played the role he played best: the warrior. He shook his fist in the air, "Get 'em. Get 'em," he chanted.

"Oh, my God," said Denise. "Listen to the Wolfman." That was one of Andy's nicknames. One of the repeatable ones.

The Wolfman led his huge pack to the school gates. We were now walking twenty abreast, littler kids were still chanting, "Get 'em. Get 'em."

By contrast, the Garsonites who lurked opposite us were silent, still, waiting . . .

"Where did the rest go?" whispered Rubi.

That's what we were all wondering.

A few of the little kids shouted out abuse at the teenage sentries. They didn't show so much as a flicker of annoyance. That really freaked me up. It was like it wasn't their time to get us – yet. And I became more and more convinced that the Garsonites weren't just after Andy.

"Make for the shop," said Andy. He jerked his head towards the sweet shop which lay a few yards on from the school.

"We'll go in there," whispered Andy, "because they've got a back way. Then we can get all the girls out that way."

"But I don't live in that direction," wailed one girl.

"You do tonight," retorted Andy.

We advanced on the shop. Some of the girls had linked hands, as if they were going to do a Conga. Suddenly I felt a soft, clammy hand in mine, Jo's hand. She didn't say anything – we'd barely spoken since the Debs saga – but her hand in mine felt good, felt right. Especially now.

"We're being followed," said Andy. "Don't look back," he added, but it was too late, we all turned round, all caught a glimpse of some figures slowly, stealthily trailing us. However, as soon as we turned round the figures froze.

It's like that game you play when you're about one month old. "What's the time, Mr Wolf?" Here we are playing it again only this time with knives and fists and planks of wood.

"Look," said Denise. "Look at that bus queue."

Opposite the shop was a bus queue of Garson boys. Other figures were sitting down. I'd swear one was the boy with the plank of wood. Was it my imagination or was it getting dark, or at least overcast. Even the weather was expecting the worst. We closed in, our shoulders rubbing together, Jo's hand now clenching mine tightly.

The shop loomed ahead. Andy gave us our instructions. "Just a few of us will go in. We'll ask permission to use the back."

But for once Andy's orders were disregarded. For this crummy sweet shop was now a life boat, the only life boat between us and the terrors closing in on us. No wonder everyone poured into the shop or hung around the window.

Inside: "And his heart stopped for a month . . . yes . . . no, no, he's out of hospital now, still looks a funny colour. But marvellous really and . . . I'll ring you back, Joan, something's happened. Yes, take care dear. Love to all. What the hell?" She plonked the phone down and glared at the hordes of pupils teeming round her shop. "What's going on here?"

I almost felt sorry for her, if she hadn't got a sharp voice and a nasty, suspicious face, I would have done.

It was perhaps, unfortunate that Andy, our spokesman, began by stating, "We haven't come to buy anything."

"Well get out then," she snapped.

I expected her to start shooing us away with a broomstick. Sure she'd have a broomstick.

"Go, be off or I'll ring up your school. I remember all your faces."

"Please, please listen," said Denise frantically. "There's a gang after us, all we want is to use your back entrance."

"What, all of you?" She wheeled round on one little girl who'd dared to breathe on a bubble gum. "And leave the sweets alone. I know this trick, while I'm opening the back door you'll be stealing all my sweets. Oh, I'm on to your schemes. Now get out all of you. Anyway, we're closed." She darted over to the door and changed the sign. Her hand shook as she did so. "See, see, closed. Now get out or I'm calling the police."

"Listen," said Andy. "It's me they want. I'll go out and face 'em. The rest of you wait."

"No one's waiting. Outside all of you," screeched the shop-keeper.

"All right, you old bat, keep your wig on," said Andy. "Come on, outside everyone."

We piled out. It seemed a little darker, as if it was already night-time not seven minutes past four in the afternoon.

"You all wait here," said Andy.

"No, no," said Denise suddenly, "I've got a better idea." She got out a white hankie. "We girls will wave this and say we want nothing to do with the fight. We're neutral."

Jo backed Denise up. So did quite a few other girls.

"Come on then," said Denise. She had guts. So did Jo who was walking alongside her. And all the other girls, waving their white hankies, as if they were flags. They marched back up to the school where most of the army was waiting. But suddenly the guys at the bus stop – and a few others who seemed to come from nowhere – started tracking the girls.

"Hey, they've got white flags," shouted Andy.

But the boys didn't appear to hear. We were all anxious. Why were they following our girls?

"Hey, you coons . . ." shouted Andy. He didn't have to say anything else. The Garson boys stopped trailing the girls and charged back over towards us. One guy with a knife made for Andy – but Andy led sharply with his right landing the guy a good solid punch on his neck. The guy swayed backwards . . . and suddenly the lads by the school started legging it down to the sweet shop and the girls, caught in the middle, tore back to the sweet shop as well.

Denise and Jo were leading, both screaming at us to stop. And suddenly Jo's not screaming any more, it's just Denise screaming louder and louder because the guy with the block of wood had been charging about, out of his head with anger after Andy had called out "You coons", and the wood was swaying around and suddenly it smashed on to the side of Jo's head knocking her out. One swipe and Jo is on the ground.

I'd swear to God it was an accident but we didn't think about that, then. We only saw Jo lying on the ground, we only heard Denise's screams of horror. And we're all raging, all roaring to get at, to tear apart limb from limb, the guy with the wood. Of course Andy got there first. I remember Andy closing his fist into a ball but his fist moved so fast I didn't see the punch clearly. It must have been a paralysing thump, though, for the guy seemed to just snap backwards, falling flat on his back.

He lay there, crying aloud with pain. And the more he winced and cried the more we cheered. And Andy gave a great roar and yelled, "Get 'em, lads." And we followed him, all of us. Girls too.

And me, I was all psyched up, hungry for revenge. Couldn't get the guy who'd hit Jo but I'd get another one, they were all the same, anyway. I lunged at this guy, white guy, but a Garson boy – who had a knife. I had to get the knife away from him. I caught his arm as he swung the knife at me and we wrestled for the knife, for hours. Or so it felt like.

I didn't see all the adults gasping, exclaiming over the teenage bloodbath. Didn't even see the police car and the ambulance arriving together. Never got the knife away from the guy either. Just when I thought I had his knife hand I was hauled up by a policeman.

I surfaced as the bloodbath was ending. Had it lasted three minutes, four minutes – or perhaps less? But the road seemed strewn with pupils who couldn't get up, were waving arms in the air, calling things out in strange, strangulated voices. They looked pathetic, unreal – until the ambulance arrived and I saw Jo, who was still unconscious, being carefully placed on a stretcher. Then it became all too real.

Andy continued fighting to the end. Didn't seem able to stop. Finally he was led away to the cop shop, while we slunk and hobbled and coughed our way home, accompanied by the loud buzz of adult voices, shocked, disbelieving, indignant.

"They need to be put in the army," said one man in a pin-stripe suit.

"Hooligans – all hooligans," pronounced another.

Andy was absent next day. Could imagine the scenes at his home – with his dad really laying into him. But at least Andy was spared Moggie saying, "If a boy from Garson School hits you, do not hit him back, just make sure you get his name."

Moggie was talking his usual crap, I mean, imagine asking someone who's whacking you over the head, "Excuse me, what's your name?" But no one dared laugh, not in one of Moggie's school assemblies. He continued, "If a boy or girl from Farndale is seen hitting anyone from Garson School, that pupil will be expelled immediately and handed over to the police."

As usual, Moggie spoke a different language from us. I did feel really bad about that bloodbath. Confused too. Had I got all juiced up and tried to act like an Andy clone? Okay, I was upset about poor Jo. But, for a few minutes, I really wanted to destroy that guy with the knife. What got into me? Would it happen again?

One thing's for sure, Moggie couldn't provide any answers. All he could do was threaten, lock us in at lunchtime and make sure we left school with a squad of teachers. But it was all unnecessary.

The war was over – or so I thought. Went with Denise to

see Jo after school. We could only stay a moment. She was drifting in and out of sleep, still under close observation (to see that there was no brain damage, apparently, which sounded awful).

We sat with her and were about to tiptoe out when she opened her eyes. She turned her head, saw me sitting by the bed, tried to smile and whispered . . . but she was obviously delirious.

We left, straightaway.

But what she said really upset me. Think it had shocked Denise, too. I said, "Poor Jo, doesn't know what she's saying."

Denise agreed – but she still looked shaken.

Went to bed early, couldn't get Jo out of my mind, or what she'd said. Suddenly about ten o'clock the door bell rang four times – really violently – really urgently. Even before I heard his voice I knew it would be Andy.

"Is Greg there?" he gasped. He sounded out of breath.

"Well, I think he's in bed, asleep," said Mum.

"No, I'm not," I shouted. "I'll be right down."

I heard my mum say, "You'd better come in then." She sounded doubtful.

"Thanks, thanks, thanks very much, Mrs Foord," gushed Andy.

Even when he was being polite Andy had to go O.T.T.

Mum didn't invite him into the lounge, Dad was dozing there in front of the telly, instead she made stilted conversation with him in the hallway until I whizzed down the stairs, still doing up my shirt as I greeted Andy. "All right mate?" Then I saw two suitcases alongside him. "Long visit?" I said.

"That depends." He looked at my mum.

She looked away.

"What's happened?" I asked.

"Been chucked out."

"Because of what happened yesterday?"

Andy shook his head. "Because of what happened today."

"Today?"

Mum interrupted. "I'm going to ring your parents to say you're safe."

"They won't care," said Andy.

"Well, let's see. I'm sure they'll want to know where you are."

"Can I stay here?" asked Andy. "Got nowhere else," he added, doing his waif act.

"Well, if you have to, yes," said Mum uncertainly, obviously hoping he wouldn't have to. "I'll ring your family right now."

She disappeared into the lounge.

"Come upstairs," I said.

Andy plonked himself down on my bed, waved his hand across his face and let out a loud sigh. Then he looked at me, "Appreciate this, mate."

"Haven't done anything yet."

"No, no, but cheers." He patted my shoulder. "You're a good mate, only mate I've got apart from Laddie."

Laddie was a dog, "mostly alsatian" breed which looked like a brown bear and on which Andy doted.

"Was going to bring Laddie, too, but thought your mum might not like dogs."

I tried to bring Andy to the point. "But why have you got to run away. What's happened now?"

Andy laid his head back on my Madonna poster. "Been in another fight."

"What?" This was record breaking even for Andy. "Not with Garson School?"

"No, just the rissole who started it all."

"Giblet?"

Andy nodded. I suddenly thought, "Where was Giblet yesterday?"

Andy leaned forward. "Exactly. Goes to Garson School,

tells 'em all what a load of racist pigs we are and then pretends he can't get out of his house, family won't let him, say he's been in enough trouble – all that crap. So these guys are outside our school waiting for Giblet to give the signal. Only Giblet chickens out, never turns up."

"And," I continued, "if you hadn't called out 'coon' there might not have been any battle at all and Jo wouldn't have been in hospital and neither would . . ."

"Hold on, mate, those guys wanted hassle."

"They wanted racists – so you very helpfully pop out your racist crap."

"All right, all right, blame me for everything as usual." Andy went into a sulk.

Finally, pacifyingly, "Anyway, tell me about today's fight."

Andy became enthusiastic; "I rang up this Giblet, told him what a bottler he was and challenged him to a private fight, a shoot-out."

"At High Noon, no doubt."

"No, no, this is serious stuff. A shoot-out, an air-gun shoot-out, at seven o'clock between him and me, alone."

"Go on."

"Well, Giblet cheats of course. Brings along all these bum-chums with him so I got mad and . . ."

"Yeah?"

"Fired the air-gun at him."

"Shit. How is he?"

"Okay."

"What do you mean, 'okay'?"

"Just wanted to scare him, you see. I didn't actually hit him."

Knowing Andy's aim that didn't surprise me. "Hit something else, though."

"Yeah?"

"Well, someone told the fuzz, so they came down, with riot shields, too. That's what the shot hit. Right in the middle."

"You 24-carat nut-job. Go on."

"Police took me into custody, told my parents, they went ape and while they were creating I sneaked out of the house with a few things and I'm not going back." He tried to look defiant, but just looked pitiful.

My door creaked open. Mum came in with two mugs of tea. "I've rung your dad, Andy, he'll be round right away."

Andy jumped up. "No, no, he'll kill me." He charged downstairs and out of the door. I ran after him. "Andy, Andy, come back."

"No, ta, mate, I'm not waiting around for my dad, no way."

He picked the two suitcases up, as if they were two feathers and sprang out of the door. "Cheers again and I'll . . ."

Crash. A bottle came flying over towards Andy. Luckily the guy who'd thrown it was as bad a shot as he was. It splattered about a foot away from Andy. But Andy was shaken. No doubt about it. So was I. And so were my parents. For the smash had even roused Dad.

Andy stood there, stroking his arm as if he'd been hit. "Nerve of that Asian."

"Did you see him, then?" I asked.

"Stands to reason it was an Asian. Funny, on the way here I thought I was being followed."

"You always think you're being followed."

"No, no, definately followed tonight."

Meanwhile, Dad was whispering, "Let him wait out here. Don't get involved", whilst Mum whispered back, "No, no, can't leave him outside". Then she said in her "official" voice, "Come on inside and wait for your father, Andy. No nonsense now." But there was no need to wait. A frantic screech of brakes and a hefty banging of doors indicated Andy's dad had arrived.

He thundered up the steps. His face was always red; however, today, it was beetroot colour. "I'm very sorry about all this," he declared.

"Yes, very sorry," squeaked a voice.

At first, Mum hadn't realized that the small figure in the drab grey coat was actually with Andy's dad. She always stood about seven paces behind her husband. Safer, I suppose. Then Andy's dad saw the broken bottle.

"Nasty," he looked at Dad as if he'd done it.

"I was just standing outside," said Andy "when this guy threw the bottle at me. Only just missed me," he added.

"Is this true?" intoned Andy's dad.

Mum nodded solemnly.

"Asian bloke too," said Andy.

"Wait here," roared Andy's dad. "See if the guy's still about – if he is, he'll get plenty of this." He swung his fist into the air and went blundering down the road.

"What's he going to do, sniff him out?" whispered Dad. Then, "Can I leave you to sort this out, Ann?"

"Well, what do I do?" whispered Mum.

"Just get rid of them." Dad said this so loudly Mum feared Andy's mum had heard. But she and Andy were watching intently for Andy's dad. And when he came thumping back, admiration swam out of their eyes.

"Gone, gone," shouted Andy's dad. "More's the pity. Still I don't think they'll bother us again." He yelled as if he was speaking to the whole neighbourhood. "Well, boy," he clamped a fist on Andy, "You've caused a right mess, haven't you. Still, not entirely your fault. This is what happens when you let a place become over-run with our coloured cousins."

Mum couldn't hide her amazement and disgust at what he was saying.

"No, young Andy here needs a firm hand, like I did. And he's seen the back of my hand more than once. But he'll do well. Like me. I haven't got any of these G.O.C.s, Mrs Foord."

Mum tried to look surprised.

"But I've done all right. Got my own business now. Earning more than all these teachers. And so will Andy."

"Yes, yes," said Mum. "Well, if everything's all right . . ." she started closing the door.

"Thanks again for your assistance," boomed Andy's dad. "Can I get the boy to clear up the mess?" He pointed to the smashed bottle.

"No, no, we'll do that," said Mum quickly.

"Well, make sure you wear gloves, that glass can give you a nasty cut. And I'd clear it up as soon as possible . . ."

Next day, Andy again wasn't in school. His dad had taken him to Windsor Safari Park, to cheer him up. According to Andy's dad Andy had behaved badly but like a man. And anyway, the whole thing was caused by racial tension and it was best for Andy to "just forget it".

While Andy was "forgetting it" at Windsor Safari Park a group of Garson pupils – of their own accord – went to visit Jo and the other Farndale victims. Then we visited their victims. Everyone shook hands even though, as Denise pointed out, we'd never really argued. The argument was between Andy (who was away) and Giblet (who never returned to Garson School anyway).

"Just think," said Denise, "all that aggro and pain and blood over what – absolutely nothing."

Everyone agreed.

"Still, all wars are like that," said Gaz.

Jo left hospital two weeks later. The wood had left a scar on the side of her head, by her cheekbone. Jo plastered powder and stuff on it. And you couldn't see the scar that clearly unless you were really looking for it.

Although, months afterwards, I'd see Jo, especially if she was sitting in the sun or by a bright light, raise her hand to cover up the scar. Just in case it had become extra clear. For Jo, the scar would always be there. She could never, "just forget it".

P.S.

And I've saved for last – an exclusive.

After the event I wrote SEX APPEAL – GIVE GENEROUSLY on Smokers' Wall. But no one, no one!! knows the true story.

I tell you, it's a relief to break out at last and reveal all . . . as if I'm going to confession or something.

So are you ready for this – the true story I've never dared tell. Until now . . .

Sex Appeal – Give Generously

According to Andy, "No bloke's a virgin". Certainly no bloke admits to being a virgin. You want to lose "it" as soon as possible. Andy lost it, two summers ago in Spain – or so he says. ("All the girls over there are just asking for it" he reckons.)

I also tell a yarn of how I lost it on holiday in France. A great yarn. And complete balls. Really I only lost it a few weeks ago – in Luton.

Luckily Andy and Co. weren't with me. I say "Luckily" because . . . some blokes I play football with invited me to a house-party over in Luton, one Friday night. So I thought "Why not? Be a change".

Met this tarty girl there, she comes on really strong, we fall upstairs and somehow go the full distance. And it's a disaster. No, not a disaster, it's just I thought it would be quite different. Somehow I was expecting more . . . who am I kidding . . . it was a disaster.

None of my mates knew. But I knew. Felt bad about it regularly.

Then one night, I'm around Andy's and he gets this dirty movie out and it's shit – looked like it had been made in someone's garage – and Andy's dad kept barging in going, "Something's growing in here", and "Making notes, lads?" and Andy laughed. While I pretended to.

It was a relief to get away from his dad – and sit in Andy's doss-house of a bedroom. Nudes (several donated by his dad) adorned Andy's wall. Blu-tak had been thoughtfully stuck under their nipples – so their tits seemed to spring out at you.

I surveyed Andy's nudes rather more carefully than

usual. I was actually comparing their assets with the girl's at Luton. They won – in every department. So perhaps the Luton shambles hadn't been all my fault after all.

Andy grinned proudly when he saw me scrutinising his girlie wall. "Not bad, eh?"

"They'll do," I said plonking myself down on his unmade bed.

"Of course, they're nothing," said Andy, "compared with the girls you get down in Soho in the shows there."

I was interested. "What are they like, then?"

Andy prepared to enjoy himself. "All the girls are specially selected. Breasts must be at least fifty inches."

"Measure 'em, do they?" I said half-sarcastically, half-fascinated.

"Yeah, what a job, eh? They also gotta check the tits don't hang down – they gotta stand straight out. As for nipples. Four inches easily."

"How do you know? You've never been."

"No, but I've read about it, gonna go soon."

"How about in two weeks?" I really wanted to see all these girls in the flesh.

"Why not," said Andy looking a bit stunned. "Why not," he said again. "Yeah, we definitely should go."

We set a date. Saturday, 20 March but decided not to tell any other mates – until afterwards. Then – what a great pose – and for me a great way of forgetting.

Wore my suit (Andy said we'd be more likely to get in if we wore suits) and my shoes with the 2½″ heel (that made me 5′ 8½″ which is the average height for a male).

"You look smart," said Mum.

"I know."

"I'd think you were going to meet some girls."

In a way she was right, but I said, "No, Andy and I just thought we'd dress up."

"Well you'd better check Andy is out of his pit. I'd like to take you down to the station soon because I've got a million jobs to do."

"I'll ring him now," I said.

Andy sounded strange. "All right, Jugger mate?"

"Yeah, are you ready to go? Mum'll pick you up."

"That's just it. Can't go." He gave an embarrassed laugh. "Cash-flow problem."

"But you've been saving. We both have."

"I had the money. Nearly twenty smackers. But it was Danny's birthday last night."

"Who's Danny?"

"Guy I play darts with, and we went out."

"How much have you got now?"

"Not much."

"How much?"

"Less than a quid."

"Borrow some."

"Not this morning. See, I came in really late and my dad . . ."

"Thanks a lot then, Andy."

"We'll go another time, soon . . . What about . . ."

"Chow, Andy." I shoved the phone down. You could always rely on Andy – to let you down!

"All ready," said Mum. She had her coat on.

Why shouldn't I go. That would show Andy. "Yeah, Andy's going to meet us at the station."

"Doesn't he trust my driving?"

"Does anyone? No, its just his dad's already taken him."

Mum shuddered. "Let's hope we don't meet him."

Two hours later I was outside Piccadilly Circus Station and following the trail of the sex films, *Naughty Knickers*, *Body Lust*, *Best Bit of Crumpet* – yes I was in Soho.

I peered in at the cinemas. Wanted to see who came out. Would it be guys in macs? Or the lads, or old codgers? Would any women be in there? Best thing about those films was probably their titles.

Then I saw what I was after: it reminded me of a sideshow at the fair. You know, the ones where you jostle down a passageway, covered with spooky pictures and posters saying "Walk this way for the Ghost Train, if you dare".

Anyhow, the dirty show was just like that – only there were pictures of girls not ghoulies – and a desk was stuck right in front of the passageway. The desk was bare – except for a red table cloth which completely covered it. It looked as if it was all set up for someone to do a card trick. Only I couldn't imagine the woman seated behind the desk doing tricks of any sort. She was young and had so much blonde hair, it was propped up alongside her – and she didn't move. She resembled a doll, a doll with a faint but unmistakable sneer set on its face.

I stared at her, trying to pluck up courage to ask her something, anything. But she just looked right through me – felt she could even see what underpants I was wearing (clean this morning). She unnerved me and made what lay behind her passageway seem far more sinister than anything you'd find aboard the ghost train.

I was just turning away when I saw some blokes amble out: all balding, all unsmiling, all wearing black glasses. The woman didn't say anything to the customers, no, "Come Again" or even, "Hope you got your cheapies". I decided she was a very bad saleslady and journeyed on to the next hole offering female flesh.

Didn't have to go far – just four doors down – it was called a peep show, only small pictures and instead of a desk in front of the entrance there was a sharp-eyed man. I had barely flicked one eyelid in his direction when he wailed, "Wanna see some girls?" He spoke with an Italian accent. It sounded phoney.

I was so stunned at being directly propositioned – especially after the hairy woman's total lack of interest – I didn't answer, only clenched my jaw.

"Come on in, see the girls." He stepped out to me and touched me, touched me right on the arm.

I ran. Could hear him laughing, but still I ran. I know it was a wimpy thing to do. It's just the way he touched me was a bit creepy, like he was going to drag me in there.

And this is crazy – but I really didn't want to go down his passageway. To be honest I don't think I could go down there ever now – not alone. I mean you don't know where you're going – nor what lies at the end. Sure it could be a nice dirty show. Probably is. But you can't be sure, can you? And I had this very silly fear of going down there – and never coming out again. Buried alive – while watching a dirty show. Andy'd say, "What a way to go". So would I, if I was with him.

Anyway me not going down the passageway wasn't totally wimpy, was it? The running bit was, though. Very uncool too!

I stopped running when I reached this market stall, reminded me of Wycombe on Saturday. Everyone I know goes down to Wycombe on Saturday. We'd all meet up in some cafe – the venue changed every two or three months – and stay there for as long as we could. What a life!

I also passed a supermarket. Seemed funny to spot all these "normal" shops alongside the dirty ones. Only this supermarket wasn't completely normal. The window was covered in wiremesh. The sort people talk through in prison films.

Watched this couple escape from the supermarket, clutching two massive boxes. Their little girl was grizzling, loudly.

"When I put this down you're going to be smacked," said the mother.

The little girl added screaming to her repertoire. I nearly volunteered to smack her for them. But I didn't think my offer would be appreciated.

I quickly moved on. When I get married I'm eating out every night – and not having children.

But before I get married I've got to view a dirty show. And this could be my time. For across the road was a large concert hall with posters for a girlie show – here called a review.

Peered inside. There was a proper reception area, like a cinema, only plusher. Here's where posh people get their "naughties", obviously. Walked up to this glass booth containing a huge cash register and an old dear sucking her teeth.

"One ticket for the, er, review, please."

"Five o'clock, we're open. Show starts eight o'clock."

So that was that. As I was leaving, she called out. "You eighteen?"

That really bugged me. "Sure, you eighty yet?"

She didn't answer. Hope she was as mad as me. This whole trip was turning into a cock-up. But I'm not finished yet.

First though, reinforcements: a really thick, really sickly, really chocolatey milkshake – my favourite non-booze drink. Had a couple every Saturday down in Wycombe.

I found a take-away, with difficulty.

"Two thick chocolate milkshakes, please."

At last! I licked my lips in anticipation. Might even have a couple more.

The assistant turned on the tap and out dribbled a few drops of black gungey water. Next he fiddled with the tap. Nothing. Finally he waved the glass, containing the disgusting black goo, in the air and said, "Sorry, we're re-processing. Next."

It's no big deal – but it's typical. Can't even get a decent milkshake today. This whole outing has been one giant foul-up.

I stormed down a side road. Didn't know where I was going. Didn't really care. Must have walked miles. Wasn't passing shops any more just rows of dreary, tired-looking buildings. As my anger subsided I thought I'd better go back. I started to march up this alley, fists clenched, eyes concentrating on the pavement, when . . . "You on the game?"

I was startled and alarmed but I said quickly, "How much?"

The girl who asked me had already walked on. Now she turned back. So did the girl she was with. "Ten pounds for half an hour, twenty pounds an hour," she replied in a flat, unemotional voice. I expect she'd said it many times before.

"I'll take half an hour. Got an appointment soon," I added, in case she didn't think I could handle an hour.

"Which one of us do you want?" She had ginger hair and couldn't have been more than twenty-five, surely. Her friend was blonde, had more make-up on.

"I'll take you," I said to the ginger-haired girl.

Thought she might smile, but she didn't. Instead she said briskly, "My name's Carol, this is Anne, you're . . .?"

"Greg."

"Hello, Greg. Our base is just up here. We'll talk more when we're there. It's too dangerous on the street." It was as if I'd strolled into a film. Perhaps this day wouldn't be a cock-up after all.

They speeded down the alley into this grey, shabby building. The door had to be pushed open, while inside was very dark and very empty. Not even a chair or a table about. All a bit strange – a good setting for a mystery film – but for a bit of nookie?

"Are we doing it here?"

They both laughed. "Don't worry," said Carol, "we've got a very nice bedroom just down the road. But this is the secret base. Our boss, the Madame, is upstairs."

I shivered as I imagined the Madame – old, fat, tough and ugly – upstairs. Now, she'd probably be lolling back on a couch, a cigar between her teeth – and a whip by her table. A lessie, too.

Carol must have sensed my anxiety. "Don't worry," she said. "Madame's all right. She looks out for us really. Now I'll tell you what's going to happen. You give Anne your ten pounds . . ." I started fumbling about in my wallet . . . "No, no, wait a minute. Hear all the terms first. Anne takes your ten pounds to the Madame who has everything we get, by the way."

Decided I'd give Carol a tip. Why should that Madame receive everything?

"Then the Madame has to check you out."

"Check me out?"

"Don't worry. It's just we get all sorts, don't we, Anne?" Anne nodded vigorously. "We have some who carry dangerous weapons and others who try to force us to do things we don't want to. Now, you don't look like one of those, Greg – and I'm sure Madame will believe us – but she may check for herself."

I wondered what Madame would do, question me, frisk me . . . the mind boggled.

"So give Anne ten pounds." I handed over two fives.

"I'll go up now," said Anne. Her voice sounded anxious. She wasn't the only one. I felt sick with nerves – yet I was determined to go through with it. Not because I was desperate for some slap'n tickle or anything like that. I just had to prove something – to myself.

Anne clopped upstairs while Carol asked me, "Where do you live, Greg?"

"Wycombe, High Wycombe." I meant to make up somewhere but my mind had gone blank.

"I know High Wycombe."

"Really!" Wouldn't it be awful if she knew someone I knew.

"Or rather I've passed through it. Near Oxford, isn't it?"

"Yes, quite near."

"Spent a whole day in Oxford. It's a beautiful area . . ."

So here I was having this really civilized conversation with a prossy. It all seemed unreal. Never imagined prossies could be so nice, so decent. "You're not worried at all?" asked Carol softly.

"No, no, it's just that Anne is a long time upstairs with the Madame."

"Madame's always very careful. For our own good. But don't worry, this won't happen again. After today you'll have a card – so next time you can produce that."

"That'll be useful," I said. And what a pose! Could see

myself flashing that card about at school. Andy'd be wild with envy. Never mind putting Blu-tak over nipples, or dirty shows. I could have the real thing, whenever I wanted. Must make sure Mum didn't see it, though. She wouldn't approve or understand.

Anne came downstairs. I could see more clearly in the dark now and she looked grim. "Madame says we've got to have some protection – as he's a first-timer."

Carol was sympathetic. "Sorry, we'll have to have some protection money. If she insists, we've no choice."

"But I've only got a few pounds left."

"How much?" said Carol.

I counted out five, no six notes. "Well, give me that," said Carol.

"I don't think that will be enough," declared Anne.

"Yes, yes, tell Madame I'll vouch for Greg."

"All right. She might send for him, as well, though." Anne disappeared upstairs.

"Sorry about that," said Carol, "but you will get it back afterwards. And we do get some funny punters."

A couple of minutes later Anne came back down, all smiles. "It's all right."

"Good, good," said Carol. Then she became business-like. "Here's the drill. Follow me."

She took me to the door, opened it and pointed. "See that white building at the top of the road?"

"Mm."

"Our bedroom is a few doors down from there. I'll go and check it's free. We have to book the rooms, see. I'll also make sure we're not disturbed for the next half an hour."

I tried to look keen. Trouble was I liked Carol – without fancying her.

Carol continued. "Now, I'll meet you by that building in about five minutes – but when you see me, don't say anything, just trail me, discreetly. Always keep a few paces behind me. All right?"

I nodded. I was quite looking forward to that bit. It was like being in a spy film.

"You see the police are always watching us and if we get caught we could be in trouble. And so could you. But don't worry." She patted my hair. "See you soon. Bring Greg along in a few minutes, Anne."

"All right. Be careful, Carol."

We watched Carol slip through the crowd. Almost before I realized it she'd gone. Glad I picked Carol. Anne was pretty, probably prettier than Carol but not as caring. Anne didn't say, "Don't worry" to me, just looked worried herself. Still I suppose being a prossy was pretty risky. Wonder how they got into it?

This didn't seem a good time to discuss the demands of their profession. Especially as Anne was staring intently ahead of her, as if she was waiting for a signal.

"Start moving now," she said suddenly. "Walk in front of me, towards the white building."

As we approached the white house Anne whispered, "Now wait there for Carol. But when she arrives don't say anything to her. You never know who's watching."

"All right. Goodbye."

No answer. She'd already sprinted away.

I stood and waited – and tried to turn myself on. Had to ensure I rose to the occasion! To get things moving I thought of Debs; Debs that night in her kitchen; Debs undoing my shirt; Debs' long kiss; and the more I thought of Debs, the more she turned into Jo.

Jo when she's excited, tossing her black hair from side to side – and her black hair shines, you know – Jo looking at me in that way of hers, Jo smiling, Jo with nothing on. Had to imagine the last one of course. But how I could imagine it . . .

And that imagining left me white-hot. Hurry up, Carol. Wonder if Carol fancies me. Lots of people do. Well, they say I'm cute-looking. Even friends of my mum say that. But to Carol, I'm simply another punter, I suppose.

Funny she never asked how old I was. Did she assume I was eighteen? But then I suppose it doesn't really matter. Sex with a prossy is illegal whether you're eight or eighty. So I'm doing something illegal – about time too.

How long did I wait there – twenty minutes, twenty-five minutes – before . . . before I realized Carol wasn't turning up. Not now, Not ever.

She'd be far, far away by now, spending all my savings and laughing about how gullible their latest victim had been. I'd made it so easy for them, I'd behaved like a total prick.

I stood there fuming, and then came the action re-plays. I ran over and over every moment of the "prossy con"; there appeared so many clues to their falseness. And I'd missed them all.

I'd missed them all! There was now so much anger and frustration in me I thought I'd explode. I wanted to hit out, not at the prossies – but at myself. So I did. I punched the side of my head four times – first two times hard, last two less hard. Right then, I hated myself – considered myself the lowest form of toss-pot there was and hoped I'd disintegrate, evaporate away or something.

I didn't. But the blows to my head had made me all woozy, and tired.

I looked around – even those drab, stale, nasty buildings seemed part of the prossies' conspiracy. I had to get away.

I scuttled down the road. Was I going the right way? Didn't care. But still I was relieved when I saw shops again. Gulped in some air, definitely fresher, and I saw a newsagent and thought "Ciggies". So what if Mum smelt them off my coat. Had to have something to steady my nerves.

I prowled round the shop, actually enjoying being in there. It was as if I'd been away in a foreign country – and hadn't ventured into a shop for years, even a crummy shop like this one.

Saw some kids pricing the chews and the girl behind the

counter half-watching them, half-dreaming. Then I heard the shop door open – do they all have that silly bell – and in came a guy in a suit. Ultra smart too. I was curious now. What was a smart dude doing in a poky newsagent like this one.

He walked over to the girl at the counter. She stopped dreaming and became alert, while he asked her, "Do you have a problem with chewing gum getting stuck to your carpet?"

Couldn't catch her answer – she was whispering – but it must have been good. For he bounded through the little door by the counter and the big door which led to "the back" where customers are never invited. So who was he? A salesman for something which removes chewing gum from carpets? Surely not? Couldn't you just pick chewing gum off? And anyhow, do salesmen call on Saturday afternoons?

"Jo, keep an eye on things for me, will you?" A girl who'd been absent-mindedly patting the magazines smiled. She'd got a brace.

"All right, then."

And the girl behind the counter disppeared into the back. The guy in the suit must be her boyfriend and that line about chewing gum "their" joke. Knew Gaz and Debbie had "their" songs so why not "their" jokes?

Or maybe that girl's a prossy and he's her client – and that chewing gum line – why, that's the password. Why not? Right now they're having a quick one – even a long one. Of course, I'll never know. As usual I'm outside while the action goes on inside.

"Can I help you at all?" Jo was staring at me questioningly. Why wasn't she the real Jo? My Jo. And why wasn't I off to a swish restaurant with "my" Jo – not doing whatever I'd been trying to do?

"I'll have ten cigarettes, please." I pointed to my brand. Went right out of my mind that I'd been robbed – until I opened my wallet. Then I recalled I was noteless and almost penniless except for forty-one pence in small change and two buttons. Just enough for the tube back but not enough for the ciggies "Jo" had placed on the counter.

"I'm afraid I haven't converted my buttons yet," I said. "And all the banks are closed now, are they not?"

"What?"

I laughed all the way outside – until yet another ghastly heart-stopping thought. Where was my return ticket. I don't remember seeing it in my wallet. But it must be there, mustn't it?

Of course the ticket had disappeared with my money! It must have got wedged in between the two fivers I'd handed over to the phoney prossies. I'd been so eager I hadn't noticed. Until now . . .

So I had no ticket, no money and was "a long way from home". Just like ET.

And like ET I had to "phone home". No choice, really. I'll ring up and say I've been the victim of a pickpocket. Act all breathy and upset. Get 'em crying. Mum'll be all right – she'll lecture me but also enjoy the drama of it all. Dad: he gets cross if he has to pick me up from Wycombe. Please God let it be Mum who answers the phone. It was Dad.

He read me the riot act for making a reverse charge phone call – told me how it costs him double money, all that stuff, then when I explained about my current predicament . . . I stumbled out of the telephone box, ear drums still vibrating . . . what a day!

As I tried to locate the nearest tube station a flock of pigeons circled overhead. They flew near me, dangerously near me, especially as I was wearing my only suit.

But I just looked up at them and shouted, "Go on, you may as well – everyone else has."

They did!

P.S.

When did you first guess those prossies were phonies? When they took me to that empty disused building or when they took "Danger money" off me – as I was a first-timer? Or perhaps as soon as they appeared you thought "Fakers". And, yes, they probably weren't even prossies at all – and that Madame, she existed only in my imagination.

So if you did suss out the false prossies – well done – and I wish you'd been with me. You'd have saved me a lot of money, humiliation and anger.

Was going to end the book here – with this apology: Sorry for the ugly ending but then Life is just an endless parade of ugly, messy endings. Yet last night something happened . . . something I'd been planning for ages – only when it happened it turned out quite differently . . .

Extra Time

At eight o'clock I arrived at Sykes wine bar and decided yes, I definitely would ask Jo out, just as soon as she arrived.

You might think waiting until the 5th year farewell meal to make Jo this special offer was cutting it a bit fine. You'd be right. After tonight, I might never see Jo again, not to ask out, anyway. So it was tonight or never.

At 8.15 Jo arrived, wearing a red and black blazer with everything matching – black top and skirt, red stockings. Yup, everything matched. She looked so great she reminded me of Tracie (from "The Style Council"), and I decided to let Jo have a drink before I asked her out.

At 8.57 my eyes nearly caught fire, Jo's eyes were burning at mine that intensely. And her eyes were scorching me with the question . . . "Why haven't you asked me out?"

I tried to signal back. "Be patient. I'm going to pop the question. Just waiting for the right moment." But that message is a bit difficult to send via eyes. So instead I blew some smoke rings.

Couldn't ask her out now, for everyone was telling jokes. So if I burst forward and said, "Jo, will you go out with me?" she might think I was fooling around. So might everyone else.

Do you want a time check? It's 9.20 and I'm going to ask Jo out in the next minute. Prefer to do it before the meal arrives – enjoy my food more then. Probably best if I just blurt it out, "Jo, will you go out with me?" That's what I used to do. In ye olde days I could ask out scores of girls. But it was all just a big joke then. Whereas now. What if she turned me down? I could always pretend I'd been messing about, couldn't I?

I cleared my throat to ensure I gave the request appropriate volume, for it would be dead embarrassing if Jo said,

"Pardon", and I had to repeat my once in a lifetime — proposal. But as I was getting my throat ready, Andy suddenly turned to me. "Does he, Jugger?"

"What?" I had switched Andy off while I rehearsed my offer.

"No bloke wants to go out with a bird for a year, does he, mate??"

Andy's timing couldn't have been worse.

"Well, I don't know . . ." I stuttered awkwardly.

"What you talking about. Hump 'em and dump 'em — that's what you do."

I didn't answer at first, just prayed silently. "God, if you exist hurl a thunderbolt at Andy or whatever you do nowadays and I'll go to church every day." I meant it too. Be worth it. But Andy remained unthunderbolted and worse, he was still yapping on.

"Most ol' Jugger's ever been out with a girl is two weeks. No, I tell a lie, there was that girl, Julie, from the convent school. How long did she last?"

"Two and a half weeks. She was well chuffed."

A flat joke prompting no laughter at all from the girls. They were recalling the old me of the 4th year; the me who worked through half the girls in the school (though not Jo) savagely chucking them, reducing some to tears. Like Denise, and . . . they were remembering it all.

Last year the girls even sent me to Coventry for two days over — can't remember her name, only the insult. That's why I'd spent the 5th year in semi-retirement and hadn't really gone out with anyone and now the chance of a "comeback" seemed to be fading fast.

Jo was still looking at me, but not directly. No more eye contact. Definitely not a good time to ask her out.

At 9.35, conversation faded as we tackled the evening's most difficult task — eating. For we were so squashed (over forty of us round one table) we had to try to shovel in the food without moving our arms. This proved very tricky. So then we ate in shifts: Gaz munched while I smelt his armpit, then we swapped round.

The meal lasted two hours; the argument over the bill nearly as long. We should have simply divided the giant bill forty ways instead of everyone trying to work out what each person owed. Of course we were quids out. Fortyseven quid at first.

At least, all the billrows had distracted attention away from me and my bad girlfriend record. And Jo smiled at me four and a half times before we all left to have coffee at her house.

And now it's well after eleven and Jo remains unasked out and time's running away. Especially as Jo's dashing about playing the A1 hostess. To be honest, she's rather irritating me. Not sure I even fancy her now. And if you really fancy someone – you must fancy them twenty-four hours a day. Otherwise it's not proper fancying, merely quickie fancying. That's what I'm suffering from – quickie fancying. So I'm not asking Jo out. Definitely.

Just when leaving noises were sprouting, Andy goes, "I want to propose a toast."

He had a gravy stain on his lapel, was slurring his words and had to hold on to a chair to keep himself on his feet. But, still a little of Andy's old authority clung to him. And everyone raised their empty mugs as Andy said, "First toast is to an absent friend – C.K."

A good toast. Why hadn't I thought of it. I looked across at Jo. Her fault, and I don't even fancy her any more.

"One more toast," shouts Andy. "A toast – to all of us. So here's to us."

Toast echoed forty times. The whole thing was divvy and great.

"I feel all weepy now," said Rubi, "just how I felt when I packed my school uniform away."

"You hated that uniform," said Phil.

"I know, I know, but still, it's a bit like burying away part of my life."

"I know what you mean," said Denise. "It's the feeling that we can never go back. Do you remember that weird woman who kept turning up in the school library and just wandered round the shelves humming . . . well, she was an ex-pupil of the school. And apparently lots of things had gone wrong for her so she kept returning to the only place where she'd been happy."

The boys started making "Don't be stupid" noises but all of us felt sudenly reluctant to go, as if we knew that once we left Jo's the links between us would start unravelling. We'd still see each other – but it wouldn't be the same.

I slipped outside. I shivered and not just with the cold. Although it was freezing and I'd left my jersey somewhere. I'll go and find it in a minute, when I leave. Had to have a moment alone – to think.

Just as well I didn't ask Jo out. I'll be at 6th form college soon with a brand new social life, lots of tasty girls (girls doing Art are always great-looking, think it's one of the entrance requirements). So going out with Jo, just as I'm hitting a new scene would be, well, silly.

"I thought you might want this." I wheeled round. Jo was holding my jersey up in the air – as if she was presenting me with a trophy.

"Thanks. Got a bit hot inside. Where did you find it?"

"In the fridge."

"I wondered where I'd left it." I felt the jersey. "It's not too cold either."

"Put it on the radiator for a couple of minutes."

"You certainly get good service here." I squashed the jersey on, and fancied her again, while she said, "What are you doing out here?"

"Thinking."

"Stop boasting."

We faced each other. If I wanted to ask her out this was

135

it, my last throw. I said, "I suppose this is 'The End'. We won't see people so much — some hardly at all."

"No."

"I mean you might see them down town — or — or in the dole queue. If you are on the dole, of course. Won't, if you're not. Although you could still . . ."

What was I talking about. I hadn't a clue. But I gabbled on. Didn't matter. Our eyes were taking over again. Making everything really confusing too. For when I looked at Jo it was as if our future had already happened and we'd been going out together for ages. I know that doesn't make sense. How can your future be your past? But you try making sense with Jo's eyes boring into you, taking you over.

We weren't actually touching yet — but we were getting there — our bodies were now curving round each other. While our nervousness was siphoning away until Jo said, "Greg, you remember that time you visited me in hospital?"

As she said "hospital" her hand clamped itself over her scar.

"Yes, yes how could I forget?"

"And I said . . ."

"Oh yeah, I thought you were hallucinating, too much oxygen to the brain or something."

"No, not at all. It's just that day I thought I was either going to die or be horribly disfigured for life and when you think that, you're able to say things that . . ." Our faces were almost touching, my body already tingling in anticipation.

Jo rubbed her finger over my lips. "Let me say this without interruption otherwise I'll never say it . . . I love you and I want to go out with you. There I've said it twice now."

She released her finger from my mouth while I — I laughed. No it's not a misprint — I laughed. But before you fling this book away in disgust — just hold on. Keep reading, please. I know you're saying, how could I laugh at such a delicate moment – right in Jo's face, too? See, I know. Let me ask you this. Have you ever watched a really sad film (like THE CHAMP) and known that you're right on the edge of crying? Go on, you have. And how do you stop yourself from giving an unmanly (or unwomanly) sob? You do something drastic, don't you – like laughing.

That's what happened with Jo. If I hadn't made with the laughing, great buckets of tears would have saturated Jo and myself. For Jo asking me out was the most beautiful sentence I've ever heard. And so I had to laugh. Jo didn't laugh, though, merely turned her face away, which I knew, just knew, was burning with humiliation.

That knowledge made me feel really bad. So what could I do – but carry on laughing.

"What's funny?" Jo sounded as if she was speaking under water.

"I'm sorry. I'm just not used to girls inviting me out. New experience."

Smart-ass crap. I know! I know! No wonder Jo was spitting words at me now.

"I'm so glad you enjoyed my proposal. The laugh is earlier tonight I was defending you. I said you are a nice bloke now – but I was wrong you're still a big S O D."

Then she went back inside, disappearing with the speed of a dream.

She took with her – my last chance. All night I'd been waiting for the right moment to ask her out. Who am I kidding? Waiting for the right moment meant putting it off. But she stunned and shamed me by having the bottle to ask me out herself. And all I had to say in reply was one tiny three-lettered word. "Yes."

But instead . . . I just hadn't been expecting her to do that, and for a minute there I couldn't cope, lost control. So I fouled everything up. Nothing to do now but leave.

Leaving took a long time. Had to hear about Debs' holiday villa or was it villas, Phil's soccer trials, and how

Rubi's gran got stung as she was about to devour a lemon meringue pie . . . not to mention seeing Andy scrambling about, scrawling phone numbers up his arm.

As for Jo, I watched Jo bid all her "guests" goodbye – all her guests but me. I hung around hoping she'd give me a chance to do . . . something.

But nothing, not even a glance in my direction.

So in the end I sloped off with Andy – whose arms were now totally tattooed with phone numbers. Andy was really high. "Got everyone's phone number. Going to get a proper phone book, put them all in. You can borrow it if you like . . . you all right, fart breath?"

Whenever Andy feels affectionate towards me he calls me "fart breath". Like now.

"Yeah, I'm okay," I lied. Couldn't begin to tell Andy how I felt. I'll tell you though. I wanted to sink down and cry my heart out, cry everything out.

I kept saying to myself, "You feel bad about her, you feel sorry for her, but you don't fancy her." Earlier on, when watching her scurrying around, she'd irritated me. So that proves it.

That proves nothing. Gaz and Debs give each other gallons of flak. But they wade through all the irritations annoying habits, they hang on through all the tantrums and rows – because they've got something worth hanging on to. Me, I want a perfect relationship – or nothing. So I've got – nothing.

At the first sign of aggro I finish my dating and cut and run. Always do that. Doing it now. Running away, running home, running in the wrong direction.

"Andy, mate, I've got to go back to Jo's, forgotten something."

"What?"

"My heart," I replied. But I made sure Andy was out of earshot before I said it.

What am I going to say to Jo? "In answer to your question

138

of one hour ago . . ." No, no, but I'll think of something. As her house comes into view I start shaking and quaking – I really hate doing this sort of thing – especially as there are no lights on downstairs. They can't all be in bed, just getting ready for bed. Oh what the hell – I ring the doorbell. Twice. I mean business.

Could hear someone tumbling downstairs. Must be Jo. It is. She's still dressed. Shame.

"Did you forget something?" A voice so cold it freezes me rigid. But in her eyes I prise out a tiny shaft of warmth – enough to thaw me out a bit.

My mind's still frozen over, though. What am I going to say? Got to say something. Why didn't I plan this. Well, I gotta say something, anything. Here goes. "Do you have a problem with chewing gum getting stuck to your carpet?"

She stares at me, totally bewildered, obviously expecting two men in white coats to lead me away. But then, a flicker of a smile. "What did you say?" The smile is expanding.

"Do you have a problem with chewing gum on the carpet?"

"Well, yes I do."

"I thought so. That's why I . . ." her smile is infectious " . . .I have patented a cure which I would like to show you. Wonder if I could show you the first treatment – tomorrow night?"

A grin sweeps across her face as she asks, "How long will these treatments take?"

"Long time. Months and months, maybe years."

Very gently she drapes her arms around me. "Do you carry any samples?"

"Just the one."

Then we both laugh as I'm half-pulled inside.

Did you get that? I'm inside!

Back on the "going out" trail again. And you know what, I'm determined that Jo and I will break my record. Two and a half weeks to beat? We'll do it, won't we?

All the best, take care and see ya again, sometime!

Pete Johnson

FRIENDS FOREVER 1 : NO LIMITS

Jez, Jason, Cathy, Lauren, Adam and Mark have promised to stay 'Friends Forever'. But now they are leaving school. Their lives are all changing – and at Lauren's birthday party, Jason tests their friendship to breaking point . . .

Gripping perceptive and frequently hilarious, this is the first book in a major four-part series about the sort of friendship everyone dreams of but seldom finds.

Also available: *Friends Forever 2 : Break Out*
Friends Forever 3 : Discovery
Friends Forever 4 : Everything Changes

Pete Johnson

I'D RATHER BE FAMOUS

"I don't want to just fade away down some back street, with Adam, and then end up on a gravestone with no one remembering who I am. I want to make my mark, show everyone I'm here and sign at least a few autographs before I die."

Jade is sixteen and a half, with a steady boyfriend called Adam and a sometime job selling videos. But it isn't enough. Jade's problem is that she has very little talent, but she knows she can be a TV presenter. All she needs is one lucky break. Then Jade hears a dating show is looking for applicants. Adam would go crazy if she ever applied. So dare she? Jade dares . . . and her life will never be quite the same again.

A warm, funny and touching story which looks at television fame and teenage life today with real understanding.

"Very entertaining." *The Indy*

"Well researched, enjoyable and easy to relate to." *Material Matters*

Pete Johnson

ONE STEP BEYOND

Sometimes you're walking right on the edge and don't even realise it.

Like Alex. He's waited five years to take revenge on Mr Stones.

And Natasha. She's always done what her parents tell her – until the day she turns sixteen.

Then there's Yorga. He has a brilliant idea to stop the hated Casuals taking over his town.

Just three of the people who don't realise they're right on the edge – until they take one step beyond.

A collection of eight dazzling stories of love, revenge, laughter and horror by the author of the *Friends Forever* series.

Pete Johnson

WE, THE HAUNTED

Just where do the shadows come from? The shadows which appear out of the air, the ones we call ghosts and – especially the ghost in my attic?

Just when she had given up hope of a steady boy-friend, Caroline meets Paul. They quickly become inseparable. When Paul has to go away on holiday it seems as if they will be parted for eternity . . .

Then the news comes to Caroline; tragic, shocking and unbelievable. She will never see Paul again. Caroline is inconsolable until one night she makes an amazing discovery. Paul hasn't left her. He is still there in the attic where they had spent so much time together.

Is it her imagination, or has Paul really come back?

"A brilliantly written love story which would haunt any reader's mind." *Early Times*

"It raises interesting questions . . . Compulsive and rewarding." *Books for Keeps*

"Written with plenty of feeling. Very enjoyable." *National Association for Teaching English*

A Selected List of Fiction from Mammoth